The Masters Review

ten stories

Nada Samih · Erica Sklar · Heidi J. Moore
Fabienne Josephat · Wendy Trimboli Roberts
Rachael Warecki · Monica Macansantos
Brendan Park · Zana Previti · K.M. Ferebee

Stories Selected by Lauren Groff
Edited by Kim Winternheimer

The Masters Review

The Masters Review, 2012.
Edited by Kim Winternheimer
Stories selected by Lauren Groff

Book cover and design: Joy Uyeno

Front cover photo: istock photo gallery

Interior design by Mackenzie Griffith Book Design
www.mackenziegriffith.com

Book production editor: Kim Winternheimer

First printing.

ISBN 978-0-9853407-0-4

Printed in the U.S.A.

Contents

Editor's Note

The goal of The Masters Review is to showcase authors who will continue to produce great work. Simply put, we wanted to find the best in emerging talent. We focused on MA, MFA, and PhD creative writing students not only because that pool represented a focused group of authors who were committed to developing their craft, but also to recognize the wonderful programs and schools that support them. The work we received during the submissions process was overwhelming. The caliber of fiction and narrative nonfiction in today's graduate-level creative writing programs is exceptional, and compiling our shortlist from such a talented group was no easy task. Our judge, Lauren Groff, chose the final ten for publication, producing a collection that is wonderfully diverse, creative, and accomplishes our goal of exposing talented writers. We have no doubt the stories you read here act as an exceptional preview of more work to come from these authors. Enjoy.

Introduction

Stories are the way we ease ourselves into our own contradictions. We can love the world and fear it with every sinew in our bodies; we can long for the very thing that may destroy us. Our stories are the flickering flames we hold to examine the darkness and beauty all tangled up in our crazy hearts.

The story of this inaugural edition of *The Masters Review* is this: that writers accomplish great things when they are both students and masters at the same time. The best way to approach our daily work is to allow the cold-eyed confidence in our abilities cohabit with the humility of knowing that the story will be told in its own time, in its own way. No matter how much we have written, we should hope to contain this particular contradiction in our hearts every time we sit down before the empty notebook or the clear screen. The ten writers in this anthology have all learned to be both the student and the master of the stories they are telling. The collection is diverse, ranging from the Philippines to Africa to a recognizable modern-day America, but every piece demonstrates its writer's patient and generous art.

Some of these stories are savage: with *Wellspring*, K.M. Ferebee has written a story as dark and beautiful as any fairy tale, and Fabienne Josaphat's *Her Dream of Water*, about the plight of a Haitian immigrant to America who becomes a nanny, broke my heart in the best way. Some stories explore less dramatic situations, but are equally vast and wise: Rachael Warecki has a rare talent, and her *The Rites of Summer* is about so much more than the wedding her wry narrator attends. Nada Samih's *In the Time of the Birthing Tree*, Heidi J. Moore's *Coydog*, and Monica Macansantos' *The Feast of All Souls* find a ferocious life in death. Brendan Park's marvelously strange *Sapere Aude* is a meditation on the beauteous and the monstrous. *Madeleines* by Wendy Trimboli Roberts cuts right into a fraught ethical knot in WWII France. Erica Sklar's *A Body in Motion*, about swimming and love and the body, made me feel as if I were floating gorgeously in the middle of a cold, clear river. When I read in Zana Previti's *The Sticking Place*, the words, "But to miss something must mean that you feel it, consistently, an ache or throb where something vital has been wrenched away," I thought, simply, "Yes."

That feeling of affirmation—that ring of a small internal bell—is the very best response a writer can provoke in a reader. I heard that bell in every story the hard-working editors of *The Masters Review* sent me. I heard it most loudly and clearly for the ten selected for this volume.

I hope you'll respond to these stories with a similar sense of wonder. The writers collected are talented to the very marrow of their phalanges. I am confident that we, who can count ourselves among their first readers, will hear quite a lot from them in the future. I will be cheering for them every step of the way.

-Lauren Groff

The Masters Review

ten stories

In the Time of the Birthing Tree

Nada Samih

Lesley University, Low Residency MFA

London, England. May 1958

My mother was born under a lemon tree in the far end of my family's orchard. Since the rest of Mama's nine siblings were born there too, it became known in our family as the birthing tree. I remember climbing the thin knobby branches as a child, racing to pick a bigger lemon than my little brother. We used to eat them whole, biting through them like apples, sour juice dribbling from our mouths. The rind was softer back then. Pliable.

Everything I know about Grandma, I learned from my mother. Most landowning women with her influence gave birth at the city hospital, but *Teta* was a country girl at heart. She was born and raised in Tulkarem in the West Bank, probably under a lemon tree herself. The daughter of a farmer, she never set foot in a city till she married my grandfather, a Yaffa merchant. That was because as the eldest daughter, she needed to remain close to home to help raise her younger siblings. She died when I was very young and as a result I don't remember much about her. I wonder what her voice sounded like. Whether it was raspy like Mama's or soft like mine. Mama said her hair was black and straight, not light brown and curly like the rest of us. She said her hair was so long she needed to stand on a table to have it brushed. I have trouble picturing that since I've never let my hair get any longer than my shoulders.

It was shortly before leaving for London to attend midwifery school that Mama and I were preparing supper, stuffing grape leaves with herbed rice. After watching me work silently for a moment she said, "Maha, you have your grandmother's hands, strong and sure." I looked up to meet her gaze and noticed, as though for the first time, a black and white photograph of my brother and I in front of the birthing tree framed on the wall behind her. We wear toothy grins and hold out lemons for the camera, blissfully ignorant of what was to come.

Yaffa, Palestine. September 1948

Baba told me to meet him at his shop today after school. He doesn't want me walking home by myself any more. He says it's getting too dangerous with all this talk of war. "But Baba," I remind him, "I don't walk home by myself. There is Fatima, Miriam, and her brother Hakim—and we have fun walking together." We usually take the longer way home, stopping by the docks to watch fisherman shake their nets out. Thinking about piles of slippery fish, I wonder how it would taste if Mama fried them or made a stew. On the way, we pass vendors selling fish, oranges, lemons, and spices. I would hate to be the one to miss out on our walk, and especially hate it if I had to be stuck in Baba's tailoring shop with my younger brother, Yasin.

Baba is never the one who tells me what to do, because that's what Mama does. He is usually the one to go to if you want sweets and Mama says no. He wouldn't tell you yes right away—even though he could because he is our Baba—but waits until Mama is out of sight first. He avoids anything that would cause an argument with her or anyone else. Especially now that Mama is moving slower than usual with the baby coming.

Even though everyone thinks because Baba is big he is rough too, he's actually as quiet and gentle as a baby deer. This is true of him most moments except when he is listening to his favorite comedy show on the radio. People in the shop next door can probably hear his loud belly laughs every time the show comes on. His chuckles used to scare me when I was a little girl since they turned his mustache into a giant hairy caterpillar. That caterpillar is sleeping today though, because Baba is not smiling. His voice was almost a whisper when he told me what he heard in town today. That people think they will send bombs down at any time. The man on the news talks about an attack on Deir Yessin that killed many people, even women with babies inside of them. Yasin talks about joining the army so he can fight them. Baba laughs and says he will just end up doing what he does all day anyway—sitting around and shooing flies. I can't tell if Baba has a problem with the fighters, which Abu Khalid called unorganized, or if it's just the idea of fighting that he doesn't like. Baba is certainly not one for disagreements. One time Khalto Samra, who likes to argue with just about everyone, started an argument with Baba about me not doing enough chores. Instead of telling her about all the work I do around the house, he nodded and said, "Maha, once a week you go to Khalto Samra's house to work." I wish he would disagree with someone at least once.

Baba says we need to be prepared in case we need to leave quickly.

"But where would we go?" I ask. I don't want to go anywhere else. I especially don't want to go to Khalto Samra's. She screams at me when I don't clean her floor the way she wants. She asks me how is a girl going to get a decent husband if she can't even wash a floor and I tell her I don't want a husband but she makes me wash her floor anyway, calling me lazy and ungrateful.

"I am not sure where we would go, just be ready," he says still whispering, his dark eyes turned to the evening sky.

Yaffa, Palestine. February 1948

I end up stuck at the shop watching Baba and his helpers tailor men's suits. I know I am supposed to be doing my homework but Yasin keeps flinging paper airplanes at me when Baba looks away. He makes me so mad I want to scream. As least if we were at home I could make bigger planes to throw back, or snatch Yasin's sack of marbles and run away with them, but here it is too tight a space to run. The shop is a square room lined with sewing machines, clothing racks filled with customer's orders and the cash machine along the back wall. The left side is a curtained-off fitting area with a raised floor for measuring and the right side is lined with worktables for hand pinning clothes. In the corner between the worktables and the clothing rack is a small table with a big wooden radio that Baba treasures more than the whole shop, so there is very little space for movement if I were to steal Yasin's marbles.

The walls are decorated with old family photographs of grandparents wearing Ottoman Fez hats and of Baba in his family's orange grove when he was a boy. My favorite photograph is the one of me standing in front of grandma's lemon tree. I am standing next to Yasin and we are holding out lemons for the camera. Baba says we are not allowed to be mean to each other here, in what he considers to be his second home. What he is really saying is you better not run around and knock over my radio. He thinks it's easy to ignore Yasin. He doesn't see the paper planes he keeps hitting me with. I just can't wait till this talk of war stops and I get to take the long way home with my friends again. Then I can get Yasin back with all the planes I want.

Yaffa, Palestine. March 1948

Yasin won't stop crying even though I promised him my sesame cookie. Yasin usually does anything I tell him for a single bite—it's his favorite—but today it just won't do the trick. We are crouched underneath one of Baba's worktables, knees to chest like they showed us at school. Baba and Abu Khalid are squished under a sewing machine along the back wall. From where we sit, we can't see their faces, only the backs of their hairy arms, assuring me of their presence.

The last one they dropped was so loud it scared Yasin and now he is whimpering, snot oozing from his nose all over his face. I keep telling him, shush, that it will be all right. That it will stop and we can go home and eat Mama's *molkhia*. She is frying pitas today and I can't wait to crunch on them. Sometimes when we come home from school I find a plate of them out on the table. I sneak some into my mouth before I even wash my hands but I have to be quick because if she catches me, I'll get a slipper hurled at me for sure. I begin to remind Yasin that he should calm down and remember that there are going to be fried pitas at home, but then they drop another one that is louder than before and now Yasin is really crying, hands tightly gripping my arm, which is wet with his mucus and tears.

I am not sure if it is because of the low flying planes or the rumble of the explosions, but our framed black and white family photograph is beginning to shake off the wall. It pulls farther and farther away from its nestled spot above Baba's large wooden radio. It is usually at this time of day that Baba turns one of the radio's round black knobs to tune into his favorite comedy show, that's when he hands us a bowl of pistachios and we know that our time dusting the shop is done. We all settle into a comfortable seat on the floor mats to listen to the silly man argue with his wife over bringing his pet goat into her kitchen. The show is funny enough, but I think the funniest parts are watching Baba and Abu Khalid's bellies wiggle up and down when they giggle so hard they can barely speak. Today, instead of making us laugh, the radio is silent, save for the sound of it shifting during each explosion. I watch the black and white photograph finally tear loose from the wall, revealing the long nail that once rooted it firmly in place. The stern faces of my grandparents soften as the nail loses more and more of its grip. I watch their faces turn dark in the shadows one moment and light in the next as the frame swings from here to gone. Here. Gone. Here. Gone.

Bracing myself, I use my free hand to loosen Yasin's grip on my arm, which is getting wetter and wetter. When this stops, I need to grab the photographs and take them home, especially the one of us and the lemon tree. Just as Yasin yelps in protest, Baba runs over and scoops us up, placing us between him and Abu Khalid under the sewing machine in the back of the shop. We are huddled farther away from the front door now, all four of us squished into a nervous human sandwich. For a few moments all we see and hear are bright flashes of light and loud thundering crashes. I am half-leaning on the wooden table leg with my head resting somewhere between Baba's thigh and Abu Khalid's hairy arm. Abu Khalid lets out short wheezes through a partly open mouth, releasing a faint odor of mint tea and cigarettes. I straighten out my back as to move away from his hot breath but notice my new position forces Yasin's knobby knuckles to jab my lower back. I forget all about bad breath and knuckles when a BOOM violently shakes the ground. We all inadvertently jump up, Abu Khalid's head hitting the bottom of the table when the glass in the door breaks.

A few long minutes of silence go by until finally Baba says this is lasting too long, that he needs to go see what is happening. He begins to leap up toward the door when Abu Khalid jumps up after him, tripping over the glass from the shop's door on the way. He grabs Baba's shoulder and tells him to wait, that we can't be sure that it's over. Baba opens his mouth to speak when someone standing outside the shop shouts to look up. I look up toward the sky to see millions of pieces of paper floating down to the ground like snow, but it's too warm for that now. As the papers land, the people on the street start gathering around. Slowly everyone begins coming out of the shops and houses they were hiding in not long ago. Baba says stay with Abu Khalid but I stand up anyway. I feel my leg starting to cramp and look down and see Yasin has wrapped himself around it. I help him up, but he stays close to me and we both look out toward the street.

"What does it say?" Abu Khalid asks.

Baba steps on one of the papers to keep it from flying away. He picks it up and after slowly turning it over in his hand and says, "We have two weeks to leave or what happened to Deir Yessin will happen to Yaffa."

"What does that mean?" I ask Baba, but he only closes his eyes and shakes his head. We make our way over the rubble, crunching splintered wood and shattered glass as we walk. Yasin walks alongside me, gripping my elbow. He is glued to me so whenever he stumbles over a pile of debris he ends up jerking my arm. I try to wiggle out of his grip, but get caught up looking around. The square looks so different with broken glass and dust everywhere. We finally get home and find Mama sitting at the kitchen table with her head in her hands. She looks up when she hears us come in.

"Maha! Yasin!" she yells out in a high-pitched voice while making her way over to us. "*Mishan Allah*, tell me you're not hurt!" She says while bending down to hug us. She bumps me with her belly on her way down. "I was so worried!"

Mama thinks she's having another boy. She says she had a dream about it the other night. I told her I am tired of boys and want a little sister instead but I don't think she is going to listen.

"They're fine, Labeeba," says Baba. "Are you all right?"

Mama nods slowly, grabbing Baba's face with both hands. She stares at him for what feels like a long time before burying her face in his chest.

Mama met Baba in the Medina's outdoor market. As a merchant's eldest daughter, she grew to love the feeling of soil in her fingers and knowing which hen would be the first to lay eggs. She mostly prided herself in her family's olive oil, taking the freshly bottled liquid to the city to sell every week. Baba was at the market helping his father set up their vegetable stand. Mama told me she knew right away that Baba was drawn to her by the way he kept offering to help pull her cart of bottles, and asking to buy her oil. Mama, taking advantage of his affection, priced it double the normal price. Knowing that it was impossible for anyone to be foolish enough to buy the oil at that price, she considered it a test of my father's intentions. As it turned out, Baba didn't only agree to the ridiculous price, but also offered to buy the entire cart.

"I was so worried about you. The radio said they bombed the Medina and you took so long to get home. I thought…" Mama's dark brown eyes fill up with liquid that she has to fight back between words. "I was afraid you were all…"

"Shhhh," Baba interrupts, rubbing Mama's back. "Everyone is fine, no need to be upset. This stress is not good for you right now."

Mama inhales deeply as if soaking in his words and turns to me. I am frozen at my place in the doorway, surprised to see Mama so panicked.

"Maha, go get cleaned up and help your brother, we'll have dinner as soon as you're all washed up."

I hesitate for a moment in the open doorway, then close the door and take my shoes off before leading Yasin into the washroom.

"Hey Maha?" Yasin asks as I turn on the faucet. "Do you think we will have to eat dinner under the table in case the BOOM comes back?"

"I don't know, Yasin. You sure ask a lot of questions for someone who needs help reaching the sink."

Yaffa, Palestine. April 1948

I am relieved to see Abu Khalid but he doesn't seem to be relieved to see us now that he realizes we're in the middle of a dark square without our parents. I wonder if he knows where they are. There was so much commotion, people running in every direction after they dropped bombs. Abu Khalid takes my hand and I hold on to Yasin's. We take off running, careful not to trip over broken bricks and glass. I notice other people are running too, familiar faces that under normal circumstances I would greet. Yasin lets go of my hand and I stop running. Abu Khalid, still jogging, tugs at my hand, sending me stumbling forward before he realizes our human train has broken. I want to stop to ask someone what happened. I wonder if any of them saw which way my parents went, but there is no time to speak. I hear Yasin's feet scrape across the ground behind me but then the noise stops. I turn and see Yasin a few paces behind me, frozen. I see that he is staring at a pair of legs separated from their body.

"We need to keep moving." Abu Khalid's steady voice breaks our spell and brings us back to the mission of finding our parents. Yasin blinks wildly and nods and leaves the scene behind. I look back once more, barely trusting my eyes. I want to stay and look, to touch the spaces at the top of the separated tissue and imagine where they might fit back together again, but Abu Khalid grabs the top of my shoulder and pulls me away. He leads us to a dark alleyway where he calls for our parents. Finally, Mama appears, squatting in the corner with the bottom half of her skirt soaked through. She has one hand on the brick wall and the other holding her lower stomach.

"Do you need help?" I ask, afraid to hear her answer.

"No, *habibiti*, your father went to find a doctor."

"Are you hurt?"

"No, but I think the baby is coming." Mama says calmly, as her body sways right and left.

"The baby? Isn't it still early?"

"Yes, by a few weeks, but with all this running he wants to come now." Mama's smile quickly turns to a grimace as she holds her body still, bending her knees in a deep squat. Abu Khalid's face turns a pasty white. He is like most men in Yaffa who learned to leave women concerns for the women and men concerns for the men.

"What if Tariq doesn't return in time with help?" he asks hesitantly.

"Then I will deliver this child the same way I delivered those two: one breath at a time." The pain passes and Mama returns to swaying.

"What do you need right now? Surely I can get you something?"

Mama and I exchange a knowing glance. Abu Khalid needs to feel helpful. "Water. Water would be good."

"Just promise me you won't move from this spot."

"Oh, don't worry! We won't go anywhere." Mama looks up for the first time and smiles. Abu Khalid nods and takes off running.

With her face in the light, I can see sweat beads forming on her brow, forcing streams to run down her cheekbones like rivers.

"It's over now. Can't we just go home?" Yasin asks in a whisper.

"We don't know that for sure. It's best to stay here for now."

"Does it hurt Mama?"

"Hurt? No. Not right now."

It isn't long before I take the brick wall's place and support Mama's weight in times of pain. In times of quiet it is so still all I can hear is the sound of air funneling in and out of my chest. In the stillness I can't help but think about that pair of legs in the street. I keep imagining them getting up and running off on their own, looking for the rest of their body. There they go tripping over other lost legs, getting tangled in toes. I try to focus on the sound of my breathing instead, but my slow, deep breaths sound offbeat near Mama's wheezing.

The silence makes me remember different days in this plaza, a time that now feels like it was from a different life altogether. I think back to the afternoons Mama made me walk the five blocks to the market to get flour or sugar. I would always complain about the long walk in the sun, but I really didn't mind it much. There was always something to see and people to talk to. Women shopping with babies on their backs, working men heaving crates of goods to and fro, business men reading the paper, old men playing cards and smoking the water pipe, women selling spools of fabric and thread.

I always stayed a bit longer near the fabric. I was drawn in by the vivid colors and I liked picturing what a swatch of cotton or silk would look like if I sewed it into a skirt or blouse. I remember greeting Um Mohamed, who greeted me back, handing me a sliver of red ribbon that she said would look good tied to my braid. I say *Shukrun* and hand her some money to thank her, but she declines and says it's on the house for the time Baba helped her. She says to make sure I say hi for her, and I promise I will. We wish each other *Salam* as I make my way over to my favorite part of the market, Abu Ali's seafood stand.

The boy that helps Abu Ali sell fish always smiles at me and I can't help but smile back at his dimpled cheeks. "Hey, *Sittna Namash*," he calls me, Our Lady Freckles. His voice is salty like he spent too much of it shouting back at customers. I say hi back and want to add *Abu Samek* but I am not sure if he would laugh at being dubbed Father of the Fish. He doesn't have much of a beard yet, so he can't be too much older than me, but his tired eyes make him look older. I like watching his hands move smoothly from fish to paper wrap to bag to hand and back again. The movement is so fluid you'd think he was born selling fish.

"What you got there? A gift for my lovely hair?" he asks, pointing to the red ribbon.

Just then, a gust of wind blows the ribbon out of my hands, taking it on a swirling journey up and over the chatter of the plaza and across the street toward a group of old men playing cards. I feel my cheeks burn when I try to snatch the ribbon out of the sky before the plaza's hungry eyes swallow me up. I almost fall over a sidewalk table in front of Ghalib's Café, but finally manage to grab the runaway ribbon, though not before sending a tray of coffee headlong into the air, landing in a pool of black liquid at the feet of an old woman.

Sea breezes are deceptive: pleasant and soft one moment, harsh and unforgiving the next. I find myself pulled up to standing by a bouquet of arms attached to blurry faces and a hum of voices. One voice instantly sounds clearer than the rest. "I didn't know *Sittna Namash* could fly," the boy yells from across the plaza, sending a roar of laughter into the crowd. I stuff the ribbon deep into my skirt pocket and quickly force out a laugh, hoping the crowd will leave.

When I regain my balance, I turn my attention toward the old woman with coffee-drenched shoes. "I am so sorry!" I say grabbing for a nearby cloth.

"It's only shoes my child. Please, come sit down for a moment."

I quickly oblige and sit in the chair directly across from her.

"Garçon, please bring this young woman a cup of coffee."

"Oh, no thank you," I say, still waiting for the heat to retreat from my face, "I don't drink coffee."

"Oh, my dear it's not just for drinking, it's for reading." Her response is in a heavy country accent, and her smile reveals several missing teeth. I only half-notice that the waiter already set a steaming cup of coffee in front me. I still have one eye out to the crowd, trying to pick through the voices for the one I most want to hear.

"You are going to read the coffee?"

She reaches across the table toward my hands. Gripping my fingers, she adjusts her faded headscarf with her free hand. "Not the coffee, the cup. You have to drink it first."

"But, I don't drink coffee. It takes like mud." Another strong gust of wind sweeps through the plaza, loosening a few strands of grey hair out from the front of her old scarf.

"Don't you want to know your future?" she asks. Her voice is light, like a child. It doesn't belong with the deep lines on her face.

"How can you read the future out of a cup?"

"After you drink the coffee, the leftover grind will leave a pattern in the cup, unique only to you. I decipher the pattern it leaves behind. The rest is up to you."

The rest? An image of the woman as a traveling circus performer enters my mind as I gulp the coffee. It tastes horrible, but I try not to offend her. Still, I can feel my stomach retch against the harsh liquid. When I'm through, she carefully picks up the cup. Sure enough, the coffee grounds have etched an intricate tree on the inside of the cup, complete with branches and roots of varying thickness sprawled in many directions. She turns the cup over in her wide hands, carefully studying each limb of the tree, a quiet hum leaving her lips as she does so.

"Very interesting. I see that your hands will carry both a beginning and an end. Your life's path will emerge from this moment. That is, if you allow it to."

"If I allow it to?"

"Your path is your choice."

I take a moment to check my pocket for the ribbon before excusing myself from the table and running off.

Just as I get to my door, it begins to rain.

London, England. May 1978

I knew a lot about newborns before I became a midwife. Although nearly blind, they have a strong sense of smell. If left to themselves, they can still find their mother's nipple, their life source, purely by smell. They also develop the ability to hear while still in the womb, which allows them to become familiar with their family's voices and the world around them, much sooner than one might expect.

I'll never forget the night my mother gave birth to a lifeless baby boy. It was the same night bombs forced us to flee Yaffa and leave our ancestral home behind.

I remember his face, peaceful and confident, as though completely sure of his decision to leave. It was at that moment that I knew my life's work.

I went back to Yaffa for the first time, years after the *Nakba*, as a nurse and midwife with the United Nations. The street names were different, but many of the stone homes still stood tall. It was easy to find our house since very little on the building had changed. Although many of the orchards were either destroyed by fire or neglect, *Teta's* birthing tree still stood at the far end, branches heavy with lemons, each as large as hands.

A Body in Motion

Erica Sklar

University of North Carolina Willmington, MFA

For my twenty-sixth birthday, I asked for a session in a sensory deprivation tank, an enclosed tub filled with water and Epsom salts. The temperature is set between ninety-four and ninety-six degrees, and because of the salt, you pop up like a cork, dead center and unmoving in the tub. The temperature is close enough to your own that you lack the sensory experience of warm or cold water. It doesn't take long to feel that gravity is falling away from you. I wanted, for my birthday, nothing, in the utterest sense of the word. And for a while it was perfect, lying there, silenced into meditation. But thirty minutes in, I heard what I swore was construction. The tank was in a regular building in New York, so it made sense that there could be construction going on in the middle of the day, a floor or two above or below.

Actually, what I was hearing was the inside of my own body. There was the sledgehammer of my heart, and I could feel my body moving with each inhale and exhale. I felt the water ripple, just slightly, as my blood delivered neat packages of oxygen to extreme locations. I could feel my pulse, actually feel it, in my wrists, my thumbs, my pelvis, my neck. It sounds crazy, and it felt crazy, and when I got out of the tub, it was with a sense of wonder and euphoria, a sense of my body's physicality that I'd never previously considered. Deprivation from the senses allowed me to connect with my own body more deeply than ever before.

I have never worked hard to change my body. Apparently, New Yorkers walk five miles a day, so it didn't take a lot of work to remain what I assumed to be reasonably healthy during the years that I lived there. I would take up running in fits and starts, and once I went to a tai chi class, but mostly I paired sumptuous meals with walking home, or halfway home, and it felt good enough.

But still, I'm aware of my body's heaviness on land. I hear it creaking; feel a pain in my left foot when I've walked for too long. I feel the pop of my knee joint every so often when I cross my legs. My breasts sway in front of me, calling attention to a figure I've never enjoyed, not even when someone called me out for sauntering in my miniskirt down a college hallway packed with boys.

In water, even in a bathtub, and certainly in the deprivation tank, that pain, that creaking, that heaviness, disappears, and I feel myself as the skinny, buoyant child I once was. There is something about drifting in and out of consciousness in a hot bath that allows for a deep suspension of disbelief. Dreaming in a bathtub is just like dreaming in a bed, except the down comforter is more like a womb. My sister used to coo in her plastic basin, and it amazed me that one day she would be walking, able to fit in a full-sized tub, that she would be talkative and snotty and funny.

My love for water has reached a peak in these last twelve months, sending me back to the pool and forward to a city on the beach; both throwbacks to my youth, and both with centering qualities I'd forgotten that they had.

It seems ironic to say that getting off the earth grounds me. In the pool, the parts of my body that I hate the most are constricted from movement, my belly hemmed in against the stern tug of my racing suit. Racing suit, though I lose my sense of competition in the pool, because all I can hear is the sound of my own breathing, the dulled splash of my own limbs. I am aware of each of my moving parts, and though I challenge the voice that is always tired, always ready to get out, everyone else in the building falls away. Swimming laps is a kind of meditation—not as deep as in a sensory deprivation tank, but deeper than any other form of exercise is for me. The concentrated breathing and the force required to push water out of my way makes concentration vital and distractions rise only fleetingly into my consciousness.

For years, the walk from the locker room to the pool kept me from using it. I was an older undergrad, and when I imagined the gym, it was like a hard-bodied version of Bosch's Garden of Earthly Delights. I imagined walking in and feeling the pounds that I tried so hard to ignore the rest of the time, imagined being stared at, feeling huge and sick. It might be about the swimsuit in particular, or the fancy clothes that I never bothered to buy. It might be because I'm judgmental, or because the women I worry will judge me are often the ones I could imagine kissing.

While I was attempting to seduce her and she had no idea, Rebecca once took me to the gym. I must have mentioned that I like to swim, or that I'd never been there. She walked me around the place the same way I walked her around the library where I worked: here is the cardio equipment, and down there is the weight room, and this is obviously the track, and here's a basketball game happening, and here, on the bottom floor, is the pool. Still, it wasn't for months that I used it, not until after Rebecca figured me out. The first time I forced her to come with me, a security blanket for those fifty steps from locker room into water.

Luckily for me, Rebecca doesn't put her head underwater because she once suffered a bad case of swimmer's ear, so the only thing she does in the pool is run, meaning that she treads water as if she's running from one end to the other. Having her there the first time meant that I knew people weren't looking at me, both because of her physique and because of how ridiculous she must have looked. (Turns out, lots of people pool run, so the lifeguards must not have been as surprised to see that as I was.)

When I first started swimming regularly, in the fall, it was just cold enough to wear a bathing suit and sweats to the pool and go commando on the way home without anybody noticing. In a space as tight as the locker room, it was a great benefit to be able to change quickly, without making eye contact. I noticed right away that I was not alone in the way that I hunched my shoulders and threw on my clothes, but it made no difference that everyone else was as self-conscious as I was. I still wanted out of that place immediately. Changing out of a bathing suit, particularly a racing suit, is an arduous experience in the best of situations, and doing it in a tiny cube filled with other women does not make it any easier.

A roaring lion's head adorned the bottom of the Columbia pool, and there was no place I could stand. The "shallow" end was over five-and-a-half feet deep, so when I took my breathers, after laps ten and fifteen or twenty, it was by hoisting my shoulders on the edge of the pool and slowly treading water with my legs. Because everything is competitive at Columbia, each of the eight lanes is marked with a speed. There are two slow, two medium, three fast (of course there are three fast), and one for families or special activities, like rehab. I started off in a slow lane, and over time, though I hit the fast lane occasionally, I became a confident medium-lane swimmer. It was a very busy pool, with at least three people in each lane at any given time. I took to swimming on Friday and Saturday nights, because, especially on Fridays, there was hope of having my own lane, if only for a short while.

Once, a guy dropped his locker room key down to the bottom, probably around twelve feet. He treaded water in the middle of the pool, staring down at it, as people swam around him. I dove down and retrieved it for him, thinking about my grandmother when I was a kid, how she bragged about me swimming all day, how she loved to watch me roam around the pool and entertain myself. Sometimes she threw pennies in for me to dive after. "You make it look easy," he said as I handed it back.

When I was young, I swam almost every day, first taking lessons, then on the swim team. In the cold place where I grew up, swimming would end and I'd dress myself matter-of-factly, either in a dressing room or without giving my body a lot of thought as other people changed around me. Then I'd wait outside for someone to pick me up. I didn't mind that the wind roared around me, and I didn't really feel cold, leaning against the handrail, waiting for the familiar square headlights of the family Volvo. I liked sucking on my frozen hair, and the deep emptiness of my stomach, and the darkness that seemed to surround me so completely.

It was the same over the winter in New York. I would finish my swim around 8:30, stuff my wet hair into an aviator hat, and relish the bluster on my cheeks. I'd buy a soda and suck it down on the way to the falafel stand. The crunch under my boots of old snow was as satisfying as the leaves had been in the fall. It was like feeling invincible, the cold not a bother for once. I liked the way my hat felt fuzzy on my ears, and the redness in my cheeks looked adorable when I glanced at myself against the glass of the storefronts.

It was easy to feel proud of myself after swimming last winter, because most days, I went for a swim on the heels of a long commute and a longer workday. I'd race back to Rebecca's little studio, and report on my swim, and put on heavy pajamas. The day would end with us curled up in a blanket, my wet hair pushed away so that she could breathe with her head burrowed into my neck. "I like when you smell like pool," she always said, and I liked it too.

Now, it is summer, unbearably hot in this southern town, and I enter the gymnasium sweating, sometimes sweating through my suit. My neck and chest are dripping as I sign in on the hottest days, holding my towel against a persistently protruding pudge. In the summer, slipping into the water feels like putting a vest on in the fall: the perfect answer to the weather system around you. When I walk outside, a cold shower and a bottle of water later, I feel comfortable, grateful for the sun, for the warmth it brings and the way I feel babied by its strong embrace.

I mostly swim freestyle, which is another name for crawl stroke. I always loved calling it the crawl, a watery dance for overgrown toddlers. It is easy to feel like an infant in the pool, and maybe that's one reason I like it so much. What safer feeling is there than of being surrounded by water, hearing only the thoughts that come up like waves? Their foamy center might remain with me when I hop out of the pool, and it might be there waiting when I find myself with a pencil or a keyboard in my fingers.

Especially now, when I find myself often alone in a new town, getting into the water seems essential. The nerves that have kept me alive while I'm driving—an activity I'm still very new at, having lived without a car for six years—dissolve into the water with the summer sweat of a hot and small new place. I've been driving in circles, embarrassed and angry at myself for missing a turn, but once the water surrounds me, the missed turn circles back in my mind, and I end up proud of myself for moving here at all, for leaving what I loved.

This new pool is pragmatic, if you can call a pool such a thing. It isn't dramatic, though there is a lot to love about it. It is not busy, and so I often have a lane to myself for the duration of my swim, a luxury beyond hope in New York. The locker room has single showers with an outer stall for dressing, as opposed to the horrifying experience that was the communal shower at Columbia. I may be coming to terms with the reality of having a body, but that doesn't mean I want anyone else to come to terms with it, nor do I have an interest in coming to terms with anybody else's.

It turns out that because I am not unusually shaped, nobody is looking at me at all, most of the time. If anything, at Columbia, people were judging how fast I was swimming, and whether they wanted to share a lane with me. I'm not rehabbing a muscle group, or recovering from a stroke, or using flippers, or learning to swim. I'm not gigantic, or tiny, or tall, or short. My hair isn't a strange color, and my suits are muted on purpose: navy or black or green. I don't call attention to myself. I like being just a regular person in the pool. I like that the only person judging me is me.

My new pool also has eight lanes, and I still like to swim far from the lifeguards. I'm supposed to hand the guards my ID when I sign in, but they've never asked for one, and the few times I gave my incoming student story, they said no need to keep asking, just sign in and don't worry about it. I haven't played sports, really, since high school, and I haven't ever gone for a run where I felt myself "warming up," but the first few minutes of the swim are always much harder than the last few. I feel my body moving, the first real activity of the day, and there is an agitation that comes along with awakening these muscles. It takes almost ten laps to feel loose, another term I never fully understood before becoming mindful of my body in the water.

I'm starting to try new workouts, more intensity, a buildup and cool down. A ladder, I read somewhere. Start slow, do a few fast laps in the middle, then end slow again. I count in pool lengths, because I am too forgetful to count in laps, or in meters. I start with thirty-six, or forty, and the numbers resound in my head, dropping one by one as I reach ahead of me. The first set is the longest, eighteen or twenty laps, and by the end of my workout, when I do my last slow five, it feels like nothing, comparatively. I've begun doing laps of kicking and pulling, sometimes stretching my arms in front of me and willfully depriving myself of that savior, oxygen. At other times, my legs drag behind me like a paraplegic's and I feel my arms working harder that usual. I wake up sore almost every day, but it is just the right kind of soreness.

At UNCW, peeling my suit off securely behind two plastic curtains is a great relief, and being naked in a place where other people exist but can't see me feels like progress, where forced nudity was only unnerving. I swam a mile for the first time, and it wasn't so difficult at all. I bought a new pair of flip-flops to wear poolside. I think my body is changing, almost imperceptibly. I entertained the idea of a triathlon, only for a moment, and probably not seriously. Running really isn't my thing, and I bike solely for functionality.

In mid-August, I went to the pool, like usual, and when I got up the stairs from the locker room, it was dark, the pool closed. I hadn't realized, and I thought it was kind of amazing, looking at the still water, ready to get in it, completely alone in the darkened room. I thought about swimming in the dark, about taking my suit off and owning the pool for an hour, about how water feels like silk on a body. But instead I turned around and drove to the YMCA, joined for a trial week, and did my mile there, getting used to its temperature, and its length, and its difference.

It was my first day back in Wilmington, and I was looking forward to my pool, the comfort of the now familiar lifeguards and the even bottom. I'd spent five days in The Triad, joining on trial a gym that Rebecca will pay for every month, and that I will visit regularly as her guest. Their two-lane pool is twenty-five yards, not twenty-five meters, and inordinately warm. It took some getting used to, but by the third day, my mile was clean and I'd added a little backstroke, something I can only do in a pool where nobody knows me, at least at first. It's hard to get used to the roll of my body over the water, the counting backward from the flags. It's hard to remember to stop, to look behind me if possible.

Coming back meant the comfort of my home-base pool, and so the switch from Rebecca's pool to the YMCA and then back again to school was not simple. Though I force myself through the locker room and onto the pool deck, there is always a self-conscious moment. Even at the YMCA, where most people aren't svelte young lookers, you have to walk the long side of the pool to hang your towel.

For the first time, someone told me she was jealous of my endurance, after I'd watched her swim four lengths over twenty minutes. She swam fast but poorly, not wearing goggles, awkward in her movement. It was a strange moment for me, seeing myself judged, but judged favorably. Rebecca is regularly asked about her body, her workout, her lifting schedule. Lots of men do what she does, and they don't look half as good.

When I finish my workout these days, at the UNCW natatorium, it isn't with a sense of wonder at being human, but with the belief that my body can be put to good use.

There's a chemical answer for this, I know, and it doesn't cease to amaze me that endorphins naturally do the same work I'd forced in powder form up my nose, forced in pills down my throat, forced in smoke through my lungs. It could become addictive. It might be already. For now, I swim 35–45 laps six days a week, and feel an accomplishment that doesn't carry humiliation on its comedown.

It's not a place I imagined myself inhabiting, not even when I felt the raging jealousy toward a professor who often mentioned her morning swim at the YMCA years before I was brave enough to try out Columbia's pool. That semester, I imagined myself swimming as an older person, old enough to leave behind my self-consciousness. Either I'm older now, or braver, or those years of therapy are working for me, or maybe I just need something now that I didn't need before. Maybe I am listening to the inside of my body, and following the doctor's advice to exercise regularly, which I already knew. Maybe I am growing up in surprising ways. It does take longer than they once thought to overcome the part of your brain that forces you into risky situations.

It could be falling in love. When we first started all this, Rebecca and I made lists of the things we were feeling. Hers were mostly negative (highlights included "ashamed" "guilty" and, "like not getting out of bed"), and mine were mostly positive. One of mine, though, was "enormous," and while I no longer feel enormous, it's hard to face the comparison of my body with the only body I've ever loved so much I'd wish to inhabit it.

Though she might argue the finer points, Rebecca's body is objectively better than mine. Maybe it's not mindful to say something like that about someone who struggles with food, with working out too much, but her shoulders are toned and freckled, and her stomach is a washboard, and a marathon runner I know once asked me how she got legs like that. Stairs, I said, and hill starts. As if I know what that really means, to run a hundred flights of stairs in an hour. When she comes back inside after all those flights, her soaking shirt over her head in seconds. I can barely restrain myself. She'd tell you it's gross, but it's not. It's incredibly sexy.

We went to Wrightsville Beach together, and underneath our clothes, I wore a triangle-topped bikini, and she wore her sporty Adidas one with boy shorts. We took a long walk, and at the end of it, I took off my shorts and shirt and went in the ocean. She grudgingly followed me (this is the timbre of our relationship), and we bobbed over the breaking waves out to the calmer stretch beyond. There was a fierce undertow, and before long, I could see she'd had enough. She'll walk for hours, but five minutes in the water does her in. I waded out first, feeling my thigh muscles working hard, and she came out behind me, dripping and gorgeous, and I wanted to take her hand, and I couldn't.

The beach is the ultimate for judgment. As a kid in southern Connecticut, I spent every summer day on the beach. My mother would dump us on the sand and promptly fall asleep in her beach chair, waking up with a deeply crimson chest and a strange pride. "Mmm," she would say every day when she sat down. "This is paradise." She would dip her feet under the first hot layer of sand and lean her head back. My mother had a rotation of strapless bathing suits, but none of them ever got wet. Mostly, they were black with splashes of color on the breasts. Her bathing suits—the idea of her nearly naked before this throng of other people—was vile to me. I hated that they didn't have straps, the way the line between her breasts was so pronounced.

Doubtless, some of my insecurity is leftover from my mother's sudden and severe weight loss, which she paired with a sudden and severe divorce from my father and followed up with a stern eye toward my newly developing body. It wasn't until I really considered the mothers in bikinis and some who were always dieting that I realized that my body would turn into theirs.

Most of the time, in middle school, I wore my racing suits to the beach, because there was no difference beyond the obvious between the beach and the pool. At some point, friends of mine put on bikinis, sprayed Sun-In in their hair, spent more time lying on the beach and less playing in the water. I missed swimming the most when the sun started to go down, and instead of going for an evening dip, we sat in the dunes and played truth or dare. Half the girls were dared to walk down to the water and flash us. I never played, but somehow I also was never ousted.

My memory of the beach before the end of middle school is of treading water for hours in that calm strip of water beyond the breaking waves. It is of laughing with my sister at pitiful sandcastles, and of burying friends in the sand. It is of braces and boogie boards and hot dogs for catching crabs. I don't remember a single bathing suit that any of my friends owned.

Because I'm a sucker for water, and because sand in my hair feels like home to me, I never really stopped going to the beach the way I quit swimming laps, despite an insecurity that made the before and after fairly miserable, like the walk into the locker room and onto the pool deck. As an adult, I've gone to a beach once in a while, all along accepting the suffering in exchange for the soothing sound of ocean, the shock of the cold northern Atlantic, the promise of Italian ices on the way home. I've gone because it's fifteen degrees cooler on the beach than it is in New York City, and a little less crowded. And because I've felt, if not exactly safe, then at least in the company of people who like me.

––––––––––

Part of dating someone who is better looking than you means wondering if you're good enough, and if other people recognize that you aren't. Even when you know to be proud of yourself, and excited at the prospect of your own life, we exist in a world that judges superficially, and superficially, I only add up sometimes. On the beach, walking beside Rebecca, I did not add up. I filled my suit well, and laughed at her reenactment of nearly losing her top, but I felt self-conscious, even knowing that most people would think we were just friends.

Later, when we talk about it, she says that given the choice, most people would rather take me home than her, and I don't disagree. But, I argue, people only want me to sleep with. Nobody would want to inhabit my body. Not if they had the choice between mine and yours. I can't tell if she's hurt by my acknowledgement of the fact that I know how to work my body, how to turn it into sex. It's not a skill that she possesses. She is a person who can relate to anybody, and who thinks faster than she can filter, and who believes that her body is a machine, and that its purpose is to do her bidding, regardless of pain, ignorant of pleasure.

I want to feel better about myself. I want to feel like we are equal, different in our body shapes, but both pretty, in our ways. I want to say that leaving New York has made me less judgmental, more willing to accept the body I have. But it's only been a few months, really, and the shedding of this emotional skin is taking longer than I'd anticipated. I want to believe that I'm not inheriting Rebecca's insanity, her obsessions, her sickness. I want to trust that what I'm doing is the right thing, a normal thing, and not a thing that is caused by the belief that I'm not pretty, not good enough, not devoted enough to physical improvement. Mostly, I want to believe that dating a woman doesn't have to mean constant comparison, even though so far, we seem to spend a lot of time comparing ourselves to each other.

That day on the beach, I thought I'd been making good progress. I'd been swimming so much, talking to the lifeguards, even. I wasn't so intimidated by the swim team kids, their long lean forms lapping me readily. But my pride has been tempered by the reality of Rebecca's body beside mine, because I bet that she'd look more like me, if she just let herself. And it makes me jealous, and then immediately sick, that she doesn't.

Over time, this is supposed to get easier. Over time, she is supposed to get better, cut hours off her workouts and eat real meals. We are supposed to end up looking more like each other. I didn't realize this was a bargain I'd struck, just by deciding to be healthy, to work on the part of myself that I spent so long ignoring.

I just wanted to meditate, to get wet, to feel safe in the water and forget, for a few minutes, about all the things that were stressful, or new, or needing to be accomplished. I just wanted to feel a little bit of what she felt, when she said once that I had no idea. I just wanted to splash around this new ocean, with its warmer water and deep blue scenery. I just wanted to look at the horizon and wonder what it would feel like to swim to the other size.

Coydog

Heidi J. Moore
Queens University, Low Residency MFA

T he coydog watches my horses. I'm sure if the old pony became ill or stumbled in the snow the coydog would attack. My younger horse is part draft, seventeen hands the last time I put a stick on him and when the coydog jumps to the top of the stone fence, the pony trots to stand beside the big horse. They stare at the fence until the coydog jumps down. The horses rotate, vigilant, facing the coydog constantly even though she's almost a quarter mile away. Only when she fades into the trees do they focus again on the pile of hay.

On Wednesday I walked to the barn. The coydog was there in the distance. A pie pan in my hand overflowed with kitchen scraps. I threw the leftovers to my chickens, and they tore apart the apple core and pecked the rice grains off the frozen ground. While I watched, I counted out of habit. The Araucana was missing. I had three of the special breed, easy to pick from the Bard Rocks and the Reds. Her green legs gave color to the flock. Her eggs gave color to the carton. I looked in the nest box and on the roost. She was gone.

Back in the house, I alerted everyone while I stamped manure-stained snow from my boots.

"Something got in the coop," I said.

My mother-in-law, straight from the city, made a sound that I usually heard from the hens while they waited for scraps. "Something?" she said. Her makeup was a smooth veneer of Arbonne.

"A fox or a weasel," I said. "Maybe a fisher."

"Such as a fisherman?"

"Such as," I said, "a wolverine."

She swiped a dishrag over my already clean counter. "What kind of place is this for children?" she said.

"It's a farm," I said and traded my boots for slippers.

I put my hand on the railing and stepped up the stairs.

"He wanted water," she said, when I reached the third step. She referred to my husband with a tone that suggested neglect. "His cup was empty." I walked upstairs to my bedroom, aware that the hem of my pants dripped melted snow on the maple treads.

In our bedroom my husband sat in the recliner. "Did you drink?" I asked. I was willing to let all his mother's implications slide if only he drank a sip. I would take the label of a cold wife or a neglectful mother, even the classification of a country doctor, if only he would drink and prove that I cared for him.

When he fell asleep, I returned downstairs. While I put on my boots again, my mother-in-law lifted the stove grate. She pulled a new dishrag from below the sink and cleaned the eye.

Charlie and I talked about euthanasia long before he got sick. We talked about the morality of excess doses while he wrote his thesis in sociology. I defended the concept, believed it gave control to a dying patient, but he opposed. In our theoretical arguments, I always maintained he would have to find another source for the drugs when he finally saw the value in my perspective. My license was too precious even for love. By the time his doctor, my business partner, gave the final diagnosis, Charlie's tumor had pushed into no man's land, found its place in the brain, and made our argument more than just a discussion. Charlie tried to deny that euthanasia was an option, but when the pain made him pull at his hair and cry in front of our daughter, he admitted he was wrong.

Of course, by then I had changed my mind.

"I'll never do it," I said. I had come to understand the value of dying, the importance of the process.

"But I'm in pain," Charlie said. He wasn't in pain that day, and he looked at me with clarity. We debated a new hypothesis.

"I'll take care of the pain," I said.

"What if you can't?"

"I will."

Meanwhile, I needed to keep the farm going. A gentleman's farm, now run by a woman.

I ordered the chickens in winter when the blizzards swirled around and insulated us with crystals of cold. That was when Charlie was scheduled to see the oncologist for the first time, and we were still hopeful. There was nothing certain yet, no insurance EOBs with malignancy stamped in permanent ink.

The postmaster called on a Sunday.

"Rachel Johnson?" he said.

I heard the peeping. Hungry noises in the background.

"Yes."

"Did you order chickens?"

I drove through the snowstorm to the post office and rang the bell at the back door. I couldn't hear the footsteps inside, so I was startled when the door yanked open. My chickens made the whole warehouse echo.

"We got peacocks a few years ago," the postmaster said. "Your chicks ain't nothing like them."

"Louder?"

He tilted his chin to the side and nodded. At the time, I understood it to mean the peacocks made more noise than my chickens. But now I think it meant the peacocks were quiet. The rubber soles of his uniform shoes drug along the floor and then stuck in place, so every stride had a scraping noise followed by a sucking pop.

Finally we reached the loudest part of the warehouse. He pulled a box from the cart. The box vibrated.

"All yours," he said.

I opened the lid. The chicks were fluffy, mostly yellow or black, but three chicks were striped like chipmunks.

I counted.

"Supposed to be twenty-four," I said.

"We didn't do nothing but take the box off the tractor trailer."

"Well, one's missing."

He pulled an empty shoebox from the shelf and set it beside my chickens.

I scooped them one by one. My fingers slid under their bellies, and their legs scissored below when I lifted them, each body light in my hand.

When twenty-three were in the new box, the problem was obvious. The last chick was trampled, flattened into the straw, its beak pressed open.

"You can get your money back," the postmaster said.

"Don't worry about it." I lifted the dead chicken by its toes and tossed it to the trash, then transferred the others back to the original shipping box.

At home I dumped the chicks into a plastic pool lined with shredded newspaper. The hot red heat lamp glowed on the plastic and the chicks huddled together. I lifted each chick and dipped its beak in water until its throat convulsed.

By the time the hens laid the first egg, I had to call my mother-in-law to come stay while I worked. I didn't have another option. Charlie needed care during the day. The kids were in school and were okay until I came home, but most nights, I had to pick up some new drug from the pharmacy, Dilaudid or Zofran, and give it to their father first thing when I walked in the door. Hospice only allowed the drugs in two-week increments, but sometimes the tumor ate through the pain meds in half the time. The hospice nurse could give him some meds during the day, but she couldn't stay with him all the time, and I couldn't leave work on a whim. We didn't know how long it would take the tumor to push through to the center of his breathing. So I called his mother. By the time she arrived, her son's ribs poked against his T-shirt and the fabric sunk in waves over his chest and belly. She cried outside our bedroom door after she saw him, then she wiped her hands together as if to say, "If I'm going to fix this, I have to get to work."

I walked downstairs and heated instant dinners for the kids. Charlie didn't eat much, and the kids were quiet in front of the TV. I consoled myself with PBS.

"Their brains will rot," she said and clicked it off.

In the barn the next night, another chicken was gone, a Rhode Island Red. Not my favorite, no personality in that bird, but a good layer. Organic eggs were pricey. My Reds were good producers.

I climbed to the hayloft and grabbed a bale of hay for the horses. A pile of chicken bones rolled off the top of the hay pile and rattled at my feet. Whatever took my chickens ate them on the second floor. I climbed down and looked at the coop perimeter again, but couldn't find a hole, a weak point in the wire, or a breach in the security.

Late that night, Charlie was in pain. I gave him another pill. We would have to switch to liquid soon. He could barely swallow the hard knots. I flipped off the light and we lay side by side in the dark, while his breathing rattled.

Suddenly, he took a sharp breath in and I held mine as well. "I've changed my mind," he said. "I'm too scared to die."

"I wasn't going to anyhow," I said.

"Even if I asked?"

"Even then," I said. "I couldn't."

He sighed, but it was too dark to see his face. He curled toward me, rolled over, and I spooned under arms that were only as heavy as the bones inside.

He might have changed his mind. We never talked about it again.

After work, I drove to a neighbor's house to pick up a trap.

"What 'cha think it is?" my neighbor said. He pulled a Havahart down from where it hung in his garage. A picture of a 1970s pinup peeled away from the wall above the workbench.

"It's something big enough to carry a chicken up into the loft." I said.

"Raccoon," he said. He set the trap and reached in with a screwdriver to trigger the plate. The wire tripped and the door clapped down. He pointed to the corner of the cage. The wire was bent, one strand broken. "Put the gun here," he said and pointed his finger, then cocked his thumb like a trigger.

"I figured I'd just let it go."

"Once you catch it," he said, "shoot the son of a bitch. Otherwise, he'll turn on you."

At lunch the next day, I sat with Maureen, one of the new nurses. She ate celery sticks dipped in humus.

"You can't kill it," she said.

"It's killing my chickens."

"That's natural."

"I'm the top of the food chain," I said. "That's what's natural."

I could tell she was shocked, appalled to work for a doctor who would consider the food chain a valid argument.

"Animal rights don't really belong on a farm," I said. She stopped talking to me.

Even though I thought she was full of shit, a touchy-feely liberal, I couldn't pull the trap out from the back of the truck. And the chickens were all there that night when I dipped the feed from the metal can. They clucked around my ankles while I checked the coop again for a break in the wire. Nothing.

Up at the house, my children grabbed my legs.

"When will Daddy get up?" Jackson said.

"Is he still sick?" Mary said.

I couldn't answer quickly enough so she answered for me. "Daddy's getting ready to go to heaven."

"What's heaven?" Jackson said.

I hit play on the DVD player and the next cartoon started.

Late that night, the tumor pushed deeper and Charlie awakened in a panic.

"I need the light," he said, but the lamp was already on. He sank back in the pillows, his sight gone even though his eyes were open. By the next morning, he was still breathing, but he couldn't speak anymore. When he didn't squeeze my hand, I stood to get ready.

I called into work and had my patients rescheduled. I called a friend who picked up my children for school. I notified hospice and asked for the nurse. Then I called his mother. She was staying at the local hotel.

The nurse walked upstairs with my mother-in-law trailing behind and she counted my husband's pulse and respirations. His breaths were deep, jerking signs.

"Morphine will take away the air hunger," the nurse said.

She handed me the brown bottle, half full, and I dripped the first liquid into Charlie's mouth. Within minutes, his breathing slowed into a regular rhythm. The bottle clicked closed, a sharp snap as the gasket sealed.

"Use as much as you need," the nurse said, then left for another patient.

My mother-in-law helped me roll Charlie to his side and put the pads under him.

"He's suffering," she said. "It isn't right."

"He's comfortable," I said, but then, as if he would take her side of the argument, he moaned.

My mother-in-law clucked her tongue and shook her head while I measured the next drops of morphine.

That night, his mother refused to go to the hotel. She knew as well as I that Charlie would be gone by morning. I walked to the kitchen and poured cereal for the kids' dinner. As I climbed the stairs again, I heard the medicine bottle snap shut in our bedroom. I ran the rest of the way.

"You didn't!" I said.

"What?"

"You gave him more medicine."

"I would never," she said and looked at me without blinking, but her pupils dilated.

"I heard the bottle," I said. She pulled open her purse.

"You must have heard my medicine. I had to take a pill." She held up a bottle of old-women pills, and shook them. They rattled against a lid that would never snap closed to seal in liquid.

On our bed, Charlie's breathing paused, then gurgled deep again. In minutes he was gone.

"My baby," she cried and fell on his chest.

I turned away and called the funeral home.

When the men from the home came to take him away, I walked to the barn. I let his mother stay in the house while they zipped him into the plastic and loaded his body. The coop was quiet when I walked in. Chicken blood pooled under the sliding door, and when I opened it, I saw carcasses scattered. More blood blotched across the floor of the coop. My hens were dead; their bellies ripped open, their necks eaten. Some were gone completely, others eaten down to the feet. The whole flock. Whatever killed them had gone past taking what it needed for survival, which perhaps I could have forgiven. It, whatever it was, had indulged in a frenzied surplus kill. Raccoons didn't go mad with the taste of blood. Raccoons didn't kill for the joy of death.

I walked back to the garage for the trap. I carried it to the barn while the hearse rolled up the driveway with my husband in the back. I set the trap in the barn aisle and threw in one hen's corpse so it rattled the back of the cage. The other bodies I scraped up with a pitchfork and threw in the front-end loader of the tractor. I made certain the trap would trigger with weight, then set it again, and walked back to the house for the gun.

On the stonewall the coydog pointed her nose to the rising moon and howled.

I would wait until spring to order more chickens.

Her Dream of Water

Fabienne Josaphat
Florida International University, MFA

The nanny knocked at the door and caught her breath, hoping she'd followed the directions down Northeast 2nd Avenue correctly, hoping she'd turned onto 96th Street and walked up the right alley. The house, she concluded, was a spectacular thing, almost invisible behind the thickness of gardenia hedges and the slithering of vines.

When the wife opened the door, the nanny smiled. She wasn't expecting any pleasantries in return. After all, she was half an hour late, and had to catch a jitney after missing the bus to Miami Shores. She was hoping that her tardiness would go unnoticed. That the wife, being Haitian herself, would understand. But the wife, young and beautiful beyond the nanny's wildest expectations, sighed and glanced at her watch, and told her plain and simple, that tardiness would not be tolerated.

She followed the wife down the narrow foyer, picking up her feet to avoid tripping on the corners of oriental rugs. She noticed that the walls were stark white, as if bleached and hung to dry in the sun, and everywhere pictures of white smiles, colorful gowns, and makeup and hugs—a pressure cooker of happiness—made her feel suddenly uncomfortable. The wife took her place on a brocade armchair next to the gaping, sooty mouth of the fireplace and told the nanny to sit down. The nanny had never seen a fireplace in real life, only once on television. She noticed a step leading up to the Florida room where the glossy wink of a wall-mounted television screen caught her eye.

The nanny sat on the step and put her bag down. The wife gasped. "No. I mean, sit on a chair," she said. And pointed at the armchair opposite the coffee table.

The nanny, surprised by the wife's friendly gesture, inched toward the seat. She sensed the wife's eyes dwelling on her orthopedic loafers, on the skirt pulled over her knees, on the unruly kinky hair she'd pulled into a bun that morning. She sank into the upholstery and felt as if the chair was swallowing her whole.

"I'm told you're excellent with babies," the wife said. "Mrs. Nerrette from church says everyone loves you at the daycare. I trust her judgment. Do you cook?"

The nanny answered yes, said that she cooked quite well—Haitian dishes especially—and that she was every bit of a mother to babies without parents around.

"Do you have kids?" the wife asked.

"No one anymore," the nanny said in her worst English. "Lost."

"Oh, of course. At sea. They told me. How terrible that must have been for you."

The nanny looked away and caught the picture of a cherub on the piano with large, beaming eyes, and hair the color of harvested rice in the plains.

"That's Baby?" the nanny asked.

"That's Baby, yes," the wife laughed. "Would you like to meet her now? I'm so happy you're here. Oh, and here comes my husband. Honey, this is…"

The wife looked embarrassed. She turned to the nanny and asked, as the husband stepped into the foyer, "Tell me your name again?"

"*Yo relè'm Evangile*," she whispered.

For a brief moment, the wife paused, and the husband nodded toward her. "Evangile, what part of Haiti are you from?"

She told them she was from La Tortue, the island adjacent to Haiti. Before that, she was from Port-de-Paix, and before Port-de-Paix she was from Cap-Haitien, and before that she didn't remember. She remembered the ocean, always the ocean, returning in her dreams. Sometimes she woke up in the dark room behind the church with the taste of salt in her mouth. But she didn't say that.

The wife introduced herself and said, "You can call me Miss Catherine, and my husband is Alan. Come with me, I'll show you everything."

The baby's room was at the other end of the foyer across from the master bedroom. Evangile shuddered at the thought of the baby sleeping alone.

"When she cry, how you hear her?" she asked the wife in Creole.

"Baby monitor, here…"

Evangile didn't understand how it worked. She pushed it to the back of her mind, with the other things she didn't understand, like the moon that clearly had two eyes and a mouth, but no one else back home could see it; like the child that grows in the womb and comes into the world and breathes, and never repays parents enough. There were enough things in her life that didn't make sense, and too many things here in America that she'd never comprehend.

The baby woke up abruptly and burst into a loud cackle. She was round all over, and waved her fists and kicked her feet, and immediately wrapped her hands around Evangile's finger. The nanny had never seen a child so magnificent. Not even on television. It had to be a doll. Only dolls had hair this fine and curly, and eyes so big they seemed to roll around inside their sockets, and skin the color of almond butter, so fine and fragrant that she actually rested her nose against it, blowing a raspberry into the child's arm. The wife cocked her head to the side.

She showed Evangile the room, detailed the drawers in the changing table, the crib and its adjustable panels, the bathroom's white walls, the tub, the plastic bassinet, and the rubber ducks and squeaky balls that float.

"Let me show you how to feel the water," the wife said. "You have to be very, very careful. Touch it first. I like it this warm."

Evangile reached and let the steamy jet stream on her fingers.

The baby held on to Evangile's collar and giggled while the wife showed her the kitchen. Everything in the freezer was packaged or wrapped in plastic bags called Ziploc, and the refrigerator door was transparent. Inside, the nanny saw dozens of bottles of water, all the labels facing forward, and plastic bowls and cantaloupe pieces wrapped in clear plastic sheets and baby bottles filled halfway with white milk. The kitchen glowed bright with white lights.

The husband was standing by his desk, going through his mail. He looked up and the nanny noticed how strikingly handsome he was, but sad, the kind of sadness you're born with and can't seem to shake. His eyes looked down all the time as if he were seeking happiness in the threads of the carpet or the laces of his leather shoes.

"You'll be here tomorrow to start, right?" the wife asked.

Her eyes were hopeful and the nanny said yes, and then watched as the wife's eyes beamed with delight.

"Please be on time," the wife said. "I leave for work early and I can't afford to be late. Here, I'll take her."

Evangile realized she was still hanging on to the baby, stroking her back with her right hand. The baby's smile was eternal. Evangile suddenly felt weary.

"Her, good girl," Evangile said. "Her don't cry."

The wife stepped forward and slid her fingers between the child and Evangile's chest. Evangile inhaled and recognized the fragrance of vetiver.

"No, she's very good. She doesn't cry at all. We're going to have to work on your English, but that'll come."

When Evangile left, she walked down the road and disappeared around the corner near the bus stop. The husband watched her leave through the living room window and leaned in to ask the wife, as he took the baby in his arms, "What kind of name is Evangile?"

The wife giggled. "It's French. It means Gospel."

Evangile saw the baby seven days a week, no days off, because the pay was wonderful and because she could spend time with Baby. To Evangile her name was Baby, even though what the wife and the husband called her was Ashley. Evangile knew that Baby responded to her when she said, "Baby" because of the way the girl's face lit up like hundreds of candles in the dark, like Christmas in early spring. Baby loved Evangile, laughed with Evangile, let Evangile tickle and bathe her, and Evangile thought truly, this was the most beautiful baby in the world.

The wife saw this, but didn't reproach her for it. In fact, the wife would stare at them longingly and sigh, as if relieved from a burdensome headache, then walk away. The husband was the one who intruded, more than once, to find out what they were up to in the nursery when the wife was out to an exercise class for the fifth time that week. He would hear them on the baby monitor, exchanging an eerily communicative babble. Sometimes, Evangile's high-pitched voice would rise in a song, something like a bird's lament, and the baby's cries would drown away as she fell asleep. Once, he came in from work, took off his shoes and found his way to the nursery where the baby lay on Evangile's lap, facing her with a large, quiet smile. The husband stood there, uncertain what to do, afraid to break the spell the nanny and child held in each other's transfixed gaze.

Finally, he cleared his throat. "Is everything all right?" he asked.

The Nanny jumped, and although her skin was too dark to betray embarrassment, the husband wondered if he had seen correctly, if he had seen her blush.

"It's strange she doesn't seem that hungry to me anymore," the wife said to her mother-in-law. They were having coffee in the living room and the mother-in-law saw everything: the glimmering surface of the coffee table, the brightness of the lights in the living room, the green plants in the corner, the smile on the wife's face as she poured her coffee.

"What's that?"

"Ashley. Sometimes she doesn't seem to want any food. She rejects the bottle, me, everything."

The husband sat between the two women on the sofa.

"Where is Ashley now?" the mother-in-law asked.

"At the park, with Evangile. They'll be back soon. I showed her how to lock the stroller in position. I think she loves that thing."

The husband didn't look up but felt his mother's glare. They sat in the living room quiet, until the mother set her cup down on the table with her bony, emerald-ringed fingers.

"How much time is Ashley spending with this…nanny, as you call her? Not too much I hope? That would be disastrous, I think. A child needs a mother's touch more than anything."

When Evangile arrived with Baby in the carriage, the living room had gone cold and quiet like a catacomb. When Evangile looked, they were all still sitting in the living room, avoiding each other's eyes.

The argument that kept the husband at bay started when the wife asked him about the one-ring phone calls on his Blackberry in the middle of dinner. She wanted to know why he would never answer, or why he blocked the call, and then went outside by the swimming pool to speak on the phone later. That didn't make any sense, the wife said, cleaning Baby's hands of sweet potato puree while Evangile washed dishes.

Evangile wished that Baby wasn't in the room to see her parents act like wild dogs in a cage. The husband said to the wife that she went out too often and should spend more time with Baby, and the wife said she was tired and did things for him all the time, like go to the gym, but he hadn't noticed, and that's when the husband went out.

The next day Evangile realized that they talked at each other but not *to* each other. She thought, as she cradled Baby after a diaper change, that Baby deserved better.

When Baby turned a year old, there were people everywhere in the house with babies and pointy hats and sparklers and cake and so much food that Evangile's nostrils, saturated with the sugary scent of cupcakes and the smokiness of mini sausages in a blanket, started to itch and cause her to sneeze. All the babies dipped their hands in the cake's velvet icing, and their mothers licked it off and made silly faces. The wife wore a pink-satin dress bought at Macy's on sale, and she twirled in front of everyone who asked to see it.

"Do you like it?" she asked with a smile. "It's Lagerfeld. From Macy's."

The women gathered in the living room and let the babies roam on the carpet while they talked and sipped tea.

"I'm so thankful for my nanny," the wife said. "She came into our lives and took over all the tasks I couldn't handle easily, you know? And her English is improving since we've paid for her lessons."

"Where did you find her?" a mother asked.

Evangile thought that perhaps they forgot she was within earshot in the kitchen, gathering trash to put in the can. She heard the wife tell them about the day Miss Nerrette called from Saint Martha's Catholic Church where they went every Sunday. How she told the wife about these refugees that arrived on a boat half-dead and who were held at Krome Detention Center until they were either deported or granted sponsorship. Some of them needed jobs and Sylvia asked if the wife needed help.

"I said yes and they sent me Evangile. They told me her sad, awful story: lost at sea with her baby on a boat, just a few of them huddling against the sun and wind and sharks."

"Her baby?" one of the women asked. "She has a baby?"

The wife lowered her voice.

"*Had.* Poor thing didn't make it. They told me her raft crashed somewhere in the Turks and Caicos islands because the captain lost control. Crabs bit them. Some died and were eaten there on shore. Can you imagine?"

Gasps, cries, and manicured fingers pressed against glossy lips. Women looked away, covered their mouths, and shook their heads.

"How awful!"

"Yes," the wife continued." We don't know how she lost the baby, but she must be so scarred."

When the women stopped to look up toward the kitchen, it was to see Evangile dragging trash bags behind her, exiting through the back door.

When they walked together on quiet afternoons, Evangile pushing Baby in the stroller, she liked to speak to her in Creole.

"*Krik? Krak!*" she'd begin, waving at the kids playing in the alley who stared at her as if she were delusional. "Long ago, when animals still talked, there was a girl who lived with an evil stepmother."

Baby listened and never cried. Evangile could walk forever, telling her tales of mermaids and magic orange trees. They'd cut through quiet streets where families walked to temple, mothers pushing strollers behind men dressed in dark suits. Evangile could smell gardenia flowers silently blooming in the thickness of glossy green leaves, and the wet earth and dewy roses soaked in sprinkler water. Behind each window were silhouettes of women leaning toward the glass to see her walk by, to see her talking to an infant who didn't yet understand language, let alone her foreign tongue. Evangile loved to see them look at her, loved for them to see Baby in the carriage.

She'd take Baby to the park and pick her up, and, holding her against her chest, would walk around the plastic slides and toboggans to watch little girls argue about their turn on the swing.

"One day it'll be your turn," she said to Baby. "I'll bring you here and I'll push you on this swing. Very, very high. You'll love it."

Once, a mother came to her while she sat on a bench, holding Baby against her breast. The child was asleep, but her face was turned toward Evangile as if to seek refuge in the fragrance of her shirt.

"Excuse me, I think you dropped this."

The lady handed over a pacifier that had fallen out of Baby's carriage. Evangile took it and smiled, and mumbled quickly as soon as the English words gathered in her head.

"Ah, thank you, yes. Thank you very much."

The mother smiled and stared at them for a while.

"What a beautiful baby," she said. "Is she yours?"

Evangile looked up and tried to dissect the meaning of the question. It was as if the woman was speaking Mandarin.

"What?" Evangile asked.

"The baby? Is she your baby?"

Evangile's face brightened.

"Ah, yes. My baby. Yes."

The woman smiled back.

The following week, the wife asked Evangile to show up at work in uniform instead of regular clothes.

"It's more professional that way," she said, shrugging her shoulders. She looked at Evangile, struggling to understand, and walked out of the nursery.

Evangile woke up every day at four in the morning from the same dream of water she'd had since her arrival on shore. In the damp darkness of the room, she'd hear the others breathing, kicking covers away, and whimpering in their own agitated dreams of water. She didn't know them. They hadn't been on the same boat as her, but they'd been on the same voyage, and now their sleep was plagued with rogue waves and the menacing white teeth of sharks.

In her own dream, she was falling to the bottom of the ocean floor with the child in her arms, dragged down by bags of rocks shackled to her ankles. When she awoke from it, her sheets were soaked with sweat and she'd have to turn her pillow over for a dry surface to lean on. She lay quietly and tried to pray but couldn't remember if God was still real, if God was listening, if God cared at all. He hadn't listened to her when they were at sea, not once.

Evangile's baby, Anaise, had only been ten months old when she boarded the boat, and during the journey, Evangile had shielded her face from the scorching sun by snuggling her under her shirt. The captain claimed that Anaise had died long before the accident, that Evangile had suffocated her by holding the child's face against her breast too long, that the child couldn't breathe under the shirt. But he was a liar. Evangile knew that. Just as he had lied that he could get them there in five days, he lied about that too. They'd been on the sea three weeks after the engine had died, and those who were sick vomited on her feet and passed away, perched on the edge of the boat. The captain, forced to lighten the load, dumped their bodies into the ocean. He was the monster, not her. She was a good mother, and she had held on to Anaise until the crash on the island's white sands. Turks and Caicos, the captain had announced. He'd recognized his surroundings, and right before they got back on the raft for another shot at Miami, she sat on shore and dug her fingers into the crab holes, hoping they'd come out to feed on her. They didn't. Instead she gathered white sand in her hand and sprinkled it like sugar on Anaise's gray, frozen face.

When the coast guards caught them on the edge of the Miami keys, she said nothing about Anaise. She ran out of the boat like the others, crashed into the branches of sea grapes and ran, until two white officers in uniform caught and handcuffed her, and took her away to prison. That was where the dreams began, and every time, she thought they were real. Yet, months later, after the interviews and the lawyers that pled for her pro bono, after the Catholic Charity Services came and lodged her, she still woke up in a bunk bed next to other refugees, always surprised that she was still alive, that she wasn't underwater choking on salt.

The husband told Evangile that he was taking his wife out to dinner.

"It's our anniversary. We're going out. You understand what I mean?"

The husband raised his voice as if she was deaf, but Evangile nodded that she understood. She could watch Baby. Baby was hers. No problem.

"Don't say anything," he said, lowering his voice.

They were standing in the bathroom near the tub where Evangile was running the water, warm and bubbly, her fingers slimy with bath soap. The rubber duck and the floating balls were already immersed, and she had laid out the pink towel by the sink.

"It's a surprise," the husband said.

The nanny nodded. Okay, yes, a surprise. She had seen a glimmer in his eye when he'd reached for his wife's hand at breakfast, but the wife had quickly withdrawn hers, tugging at her napkin and spreading it on her lap without a word. The wife barely spoke to him. Evangile thought this odd, because back in her country, when she herself withdrew from men, it was always with a smile or a joke. She did it to be coy, but the wife did it out of bitterness. It was clear. There was a hinging in her jaw when she ignored her husband and turned her attention to Baby, who had her mouth open wide for the breakfast Evangile was feeding her.

The water was warm to the touch and Evangile let it run on her fingers and on Baby's round, calabash-shaped head. The water lacquered Baby's hair to her head and her eyes fluttered when she tried to hold her breath and water dripped into her mouth.

"Don't be scared," Evangile whispered.

Baby started to fuss, the cry rising from her mouth in a broken staccato. Evangile poured more water, softly and slowly touching her translucent skin with the tip of her fingers. Sitting in the tub, Baby's head and shoulders emerged from the bubbles like mountains in the great Biblical flood. Evangile pushed the rubber duck toward her but she didn't seem interested. She continued her soft cry.

Evangile shook her head slowly.

"*Pa kriye*," she said. "Don't cry."

Baby's eyes were narrow slits behind a thick grid of wet lashes. She didn't like the water pouring on her face. Evangile understood that. Babies were not meant for the water. No one was meant for the water. When her Anaise cried at sea, the other occupants on the boat were not happy about it. Someone said she shouldn't have brought the baby with her, that it was insanity. Another person said, "*Voye'l jete!* Get rid of it, throw it in the water!"

Evangile had shouted at the man.

"You don't have any heart in you!" she yelled. "She's just a baby."

"You can't take babies on a journey like this," another responded. "It's madness."

Evangile was not mad. She wanted everything that was good for her and for her baby, and that's why she was on the boat. That's why it was important to go "*lòt bò dlo*," away from the guns and the fire that had eaten away at her convenience store and robbed her parents of their sanity at such an old age. Anaise deserved better, and Evangile needed her to remain strong for the voyage at sea. But Anaise's face was charred in the furnace of the sun like the back of her mother's neck and arms, and her small lips were scabbed. Evangile rubbed them with seawater but it burned, and Anaise cried like Baby was crying now, the cries drowning out in the crepuscule.

The boat swayed at first, gently, as she kept Anaise's face covered under her shirt. Anaise had stopped crying altogether and it was good, it was a relief, because the others had started to shoot her angry, murderous looks. Evangile had won the battle and blessed the rocking of the boat for appeasing her daughter's cries. But when she'd lifted her shirt, the color had drained from Anaise's face. She seemed petrified and limp, pale under the ebb of daylight.

"You killed her," a woman whispered, tucked in the back of the boat, her mouth crusted with salt and vomit.

"No. No," Evangile murmured, shaking her head vehemently. "No. She's fine. It's all right."

And she held on to Anaise, for days, feeding her with what was left in her breast, humming songs that played in her brain on a loop.

"*Dodo Titit*, sleep Mommy's little one. If you don't, *krab la va manje'w*. You'll be eaten by the big bad crab."

Evangile gasped at the memory, and when she closed her mouth, the taste of the sea was there, lodged under her tongue. By then Baby had stopped crying.

The wife didn't go to the burial. Her family, being strictly Haitian, said it was bad luck for a young woman to witness the moment her child was lowered into the ground. If she did, all her children would come to die. She argued that it was fine, that there could be no other children after this, but they insisted, cajoled her, pressed their hands on her shoulder and whispered words to her in French.

"Courage," they said. "Be strong."

She looked at her husband as he watched the coffin being loaded into the hearse. She couldn't see his face but she knew he was crying. He had been crying since that night, when they came back from dinner, half-drunk and half-angry, to find Evangile perched over the tub, her hand pressing down on Baby's chest to keep her still under the water. He had almost strangled Evangile, but the police arrived, alerted by neighbors who had heard the wife's frantic cries. When they handcuffed the nanny and dragged her away, the husband cried. When they strapped Baby's inert body onto the gurney and zipped it in the bag, the husband cried. And when he followed the ambulance down the street in his car, he was still crying.

"She's my baby," the wife said as he got into his car. "I have to go." But the husband did not respond. Finally, someone dragged her to a town car.

The husband went to the cemetery. He sprinkled a handful of fresh dirt and rose petals on the little black coffin before it lowered in the hole. And still he cried. The wife stayed home with relatives and stared into the empty fireplace that had never been lit in the Miami heat. Someone made her a special grief tea, Verveine, and she found it interesting. In the midst of the darkness that consumed her, it left the taste and sharpness of sea salt under her tongue.

Madeleines

Wendy Trimboli Roberts
Vermont College of Fine Arts, Low Residency MFA

Untersturmführer Feldheim crested the hill in a rush of weightlessness, snowy fields swelling out before him like the inflated domes of parachute canopies. A lone building hunkered in the valley below. In the graying dawn light, he could just make out the painted script *Hotel des Ardenne*s that stretched across the front of the building. Something white draped from one of the upper windows, a curtain perhaps, tied to the window struts as a makeshift flag. The fabric swung stiffly in the breeze.

He parked his dilapidated staff car on the street outside; it looked as if someone had beaten the hood with a rifle butt. He shouldn't have stopped at all, but he'd spent the entire night in an abandoned classroom in some Belgian village—he'd already forgotten the name—drafting dispatches by punching the typewriter with two fingers, pausing only to stoke the fire with his mistakes when his hands grew numb. Coffee, he reasoned, even bad coffee, might make the difference between a successful trip to the front lines and his lying dead in some goddamn foreign ditch.

After scraping the worst of the muck from his soles on the metal wedge bolted to the front step—how appropriate for this mud hole—he swung the door and clomped inside. At least it was warmer here, somehow, though no fire burned in the hearth. The leather straps of his courier satchel creaked on their metal rings. The clink of buckles and harness and holster punctuated his every step so that he sounded like some rhythmic, efficient machine. So he hoped. Then his boot caught on a rill in the well-worn floor and he stumbled forward, jangling like a dropped handful of coins. He fetched his cap from the floor. For once no one laughed. No one was there to see.

Vacant tables clustered near the windows among splotches of milky half-light, their rough-hewn legs at odds with the spindly chairs like a crew of ditch diggers among ballerinas. Above Feldheim's head the ancient ceiling sagged, the rafters so low he could have clasped his palms around one, even done a dozen chin-ups if he'd been drunk enough and egged on by friends. The café's walls had been recently whitewashed in an effort to brighten the long, low room, but the chemical tang of the lime couldn't cover the earthy, soured smell of forsaken food from a disused kitchen. On a side table beneath one window a phonograph record spun out some familiar Schubert melody.

A woman in an apron appeared behind the bar. She must have heard his clanking entrance after all because she materialized from the back room—or perhaps thin air—before he had to shout for someone to fetch him a *café au lait*. Her face bore a flustered expression, lips parted, and strands of hair stuck to her forehead. He had hoped there would be a woman, and so he flirted with her the way he flirted with most women who were neither too old nor too ugly.

He leaned toward her with a smile, elbows on the bar, and twisted his coins between fingers and thumb. "I'm surprised you haven't closed up," he said in French. "You can hear the artillery from here." He tilted his head as he spoke and dropped one shoulder to ensure she didn't miss his lieutenant's rank, or the glittering SS hash marks on his collar.

"Can you, monsieur?" The woman poured him the usual coffee-like substance made of chicory and roasted barley. "I prefer not to listen anymore. Or I should have closed up long ago."

"Then I'll drink to your bravery, mademoiselle." Feldheim overpaid, sliding the coins toward her. They scraped the bar with a sound like sled runners crossing ice. As she counted the coins with her eyes, her lips moved, *dix, vingt, trente*. She moved to sweep the coins into her apron pocket, extending a hand that Feldheim caught and pressed between his palms. Her face whirled toward him, as if set in motion by the leverage of his hands, and he pulled her closer until her apron met the counter and her wide eyes locked for a second with his. She smiled, and Feldheim realized she was quite beautiful; she just hid it well. He released her hand, and she let him slip the coins into her apron pocket.

"And you are…*panzer*?" She held her hand up like a tank turret. "You fire the big cannons?"

"Yes," he said. It was only a half-lie. Feldheim had trained to command a Mark V Panther tank. He had even led field exercises in southern France until early June, when the commander of the 2nd SS *Panzer* Regiment requested him by name after the previous adjutant broke his neck in a motorcycle accident. Feldheim desperately wanted to believe that his stellar records and suave political demeanor had caught the regimental commander's notice. In truth, he'd only distinguished himself in some swanky Toulouse hotel bar, emboldened after half a dozen rounds of schnapps, by accepting his commander's challenge to a game of chess and, by some lucky accident, beating him.

Though the other officers took pleasure in reminding him of this crowning moment of military prowess, Feldheim's memory of that night contained only blurry, sporadic images: the checkmated king prostrate before him, the chandeliers that throbbed as his cheering comrades heaved him skyward in their arms, and the vast crimson carpet on which he awoke the next morning, still clutching the table's leg like a scepter. Throughout the evening he must have decorated the cocktail menu with a procession of topless women because, on the day he was first shown to his adjutant's post, there it stood, propped open on the desk. The "U" in MENU buttressed half the bosom of one girl who seemed to lean toward him, blowing a kiss.

"A tactician and an artist," the commander had said over his shoulder as Feldheim faced his adjutant's desk for the first time. "Your mother must faint with pride." The old man perhaps detected the droop of Feldheim's shoulders because he continued, not unkindly, "Your peers often think of this post as punishment, but that is not the case. Name any colonel, any general; they filtered up through the ranks with the help of the superiors they served. Serve me well, young man, and I may clear some stones from your path." He handed Feldheim a sheaf of papers. "My correspondence. I hope you type as well as you draw. If you can't read my handwriting, ask the orderly. The first letter is for my wife. No doodling in the margins."

For six months Feldheim managed to make himself indispensable. Though his tactical genius remained untapped, his editorial assistance ensured that a) the commander's wife could read her husband's letters without cryptological assistance and b) she would not assail him with brusque responses, anger unconcealed by her looping cursive, to demand if dear August still loved her and missed the children, or could only those damnable Panthers hold his attention these days? For months Feldheim shredded and redrafted his commander's fumbling attempts to soothe her. Feldheim should have returned to the line at the beginning of December, but the commander, citing the difficulties of staff changeovers during this latest winter assault in the Belgian Ardennes, had filed a month-long extension. On the first of January, 1945, *Untersturmführer* Feldheim would be free again to command a Panther of his own. But for now he only commanded this white-aproned woman's attention.

"Of course I fire the big cannons." He winked at the woman and leaned close. "Mine's the biggest."

The woman turned away, but not before he saw the scarlet rise in her cheeks. He thought he had gone too far, but she made a sound that could have been a stifled giggle and produced an unlabeled bottle from a recess under the bar. She added a slosh of clear liquid to his coffee.

Feldheim nodded and smiled at her again, raising his eyes. "I take it alcohol is more plentiful than cream these days?" he asked.

The woman gave a forced, dry laugh. She reddened again, but this time she tucked her shoulders back. "You want the brandy, then you want the cream."

"I never asked for brandy. You chose to give it to me. Now I'm asking for the cream."

"Very good, very good." The woman fanned her face with her hand. "Next you will want a veal cutlet with gravy. Then you will have to provide the calf yourself." She waved him toward the tables but he shook his head. He had a schedule. He would stand and wait for his cream. Then he would leave, though he might come back later.

She'd splashed coffee on the bar by accident, and now he'd smeared it with his elbow. He blotted his sleeve with his handkerchief and slid to a drier stretch of countertop, brushing aside a few salt grains that dusted its surface. The woman at last brought out a cruet of lumpy cream.

"Cream is plentiful enough," she said, a hard note of pride in her voice. "I have no sugar. Not for weeks." She pursed her lips, as if this might somehow vouch for her honor. "Weeks."

Feldheim shrugged to pretend he didn't care one way or another. He licked one fingertip and pressed it into a constellation of the white grains in front of him. The woman sucked on her lower lip. She swiped a damp cloth along the bar, but it was too late. Her eyes followed Feldheim's finger as he touched it to his tongue. There was never any sugar at cafés like these, or so they'd have him believe. She probably had burlap sacks of it in the cellar, big leaking sacks, white dunes of sugar half a meter high that children could sled down.

He had no time to search the cellar, but she wouldn't know that. He dimmed the smile and flicked the sugar on his finger at her face. She blinked it away in confusion. Sometimes when he didn't read them carefully they'd burst into tears, but no, this one just laid one palm across her bosom and sighed defeat.

"Sugar for monsieur." Her posture deflated. She excused herself to the back room and returned with the lopsided lump of an embroidered pillow, top seam ripped out, its innards stuffed with sugar. She handed him a soupspoon as if she expected him to shovel sugar into his mouth and pockets, too.

Feldheim scooped a coin-sized lump into his cup. He could have all the sugar he wanted, except that what he really wanted from her was strictly forbidden. The orders in his courier bag dragged at his shoulder. He needed to leave. He stood at the bar and sipped the coffee as fast as he could without scalding his mouth while the woman avoided him by polishing spoons with a frayed terrycloth. The kettle trilled, spewing steam that she batted with her cloth. She shimmered in the vapor as if she might fade away in a puff.

He allowed himself to smile again and stirred his coffee in time to the scratchy orchestra wafting from the phonograph. The woman had turned her back. Cup and saucer in hand, Feldheim moved to the phonograph by the window. He had guessed right, Schubert.

The woman spoke. "The music is nice, yes?"

Feldheim nodded. "All the best melodies are in minor key." He lifted the needle to play the song again.

Pushing aside the yellowed-lace curtain, he looked outside. No snow falling yet, though patches of it crusted the ground. He hoped the weather would hold long enough for his drive to the lines and back. First blue sky in days, soon to be crosshatched with contrails when the planes arrived. Better snow than planes. He should have skipped the coffee and come here to eat on the way back instead. Still could.

Vapor vented from a battle-weary convoy milling in the field across the road. A squad of Waffen-SS mechanized infantry took turns sitting on the hoods of their idling vehicles to warm themselves—presumably the rest had run out of fuel—and guarded a cluster of about a dozen prisoners. The SS men shifted in their camouflage parkas and wraps made of waterproof tent-halves. They had stomped narrow paths through the snowy field, interlocking circles around a huddle of Allied prisoners.

Feldheim glanced back at the woman, her shoulders hunched, as she glided behind the bar in an eerie silence, perhaps in fur slippers although he couldn't see her feet. She wiped a stack of tumblers with her cloth and watched him through the bottom of each cup, her face distorted by the thick glass. Sometimes she stopped and tilted her head, listening for something above the music, something Feldheim couldn't hear and that he knew must be her children, probably asleep upstairs.

As Feldheim moved to let the curtain fall he heard a rumble like snow falling off a roof. The snout of a Panther tank nosed over the hill. It roared down the road and across a narrow stone bridge without slowing, surprising Feldheim by not tumbling into the creek. As it approached the café the Panther slowed, then halted less than a meter behind Feldheim's own sorry-looking piece of scrap slouched out front. The infantrymen in the field turned their heads to stare. The Panther's commander, a field-grade officer by the smear of gold on his epaulets, surveyed them for a moment, then sprung from the upper hatch. Although Feldheim couldn't quite make out the officer's face now that he'd leaned too close and fogged up the window, he knew by the man's confident gait that it was the new battalion commander, Major Weiss.

Feldheim let the curtain fall. He contemplated escape out the back door, wherever it was, but only had time to straighten his collar and run a hand through his hair before the major burst through the door. The major's compact, athletic build suggested a passion for boxing, further evidenced by the mangled cartilage of his left ear. His face had solidified into a dour mask, and purple blotches of fatigue ringed his eyes like bruises.

"*Untersturmführer* Feldheim!" Weiss addressed Feldheim in the same manner he might call for a waiter who had pretended not to notice him. The major must have sought him out personally after recognizing the car out front. "Why are there idle infantrymen scratching their balls in that fucking field?"

"With respect, *Sturmbannführer*," said Feldheim as calmly as he could manage, "those infantrymen report to a different regiment entirely." His eyes followed the line of muddy footmarks speckling the floor behind the major like some distress call in Morse code.

"I don't care if you're a pilot who bailed out of his fucking plane. As an officer I'd expect you to boot their asses to the front where they belong. Getting a good scratch, are we?"

"My apologies, *Sturmbannführer*. I didn't realize I had broken any rules. With your permission I'll be on my way."

"Permission denied. On your way where?"

"To the front line, *Sturmbannführer*. I'm acting on the orders of the regimental commander—"

The major's eyes bulged. "Don't you flash rank you don't have around me. Does this look like the front to you? Do you think your desk job entitles you to muck about with no sense of urgency?"

Acidic guilt bloomed in Feldheim's stomach. Weiss had called his honor into question, and now Feldheim stood before him, immobilized, vulnerable as a man tied before the firing squad. All he needed was a blindfold. The commander wouldn't have cared if Feldheim stopped at a café, as long as the job got done. Weiss was not the commander.

"Better men have been shot for shirking duty."

"Beg to report, *Sturmbannführer*, I know. Forgive me, it will never happen again."

"My God, what a night," said Weiss in a low, tired voice. "I lost one of my crews. Molotov cocktail through the hatch. I'm surprised the partisans haven't firebombed you too, standing in the fucking window with your coffee."

"I hope you're not too disappointed, *Sturmbannführer*."

The woman's shadow flickered beneath the door to the back room where she had fled. It didn't matter if she didn't understand German. Feldheim wondered if she leaned there against the door, laughing at the sounds of his disgrace.

"Who's there?" Weiss pointed at the shadow.

"Beg to report, she's just the proprietor—"

"She? And I trust she's tolerable to look at?"

"I…yes, *Sturmbannführer*. Tolerable. "

The major smirked. "Well? Call her out, then."

Feldheim reluctantly did as he was told. The woman hurried over, her terrycloth slung across one shoulder like a sash. She caught Feldheim's eye as she set a dish of crumbled madeleines on the bar. "Found them in a tin just now," she mumbled in French between nervous gulps of air. "Swore it was empty. May I tempt messieurs?"

"I'd do her if I had a desk job and nothing else to do." Weiss raised an eyebrow at Feldheim, who crammed a madeleine in his mouth. "So, what did she say? Oh what the hell. Tell her to get me whatever you had. A mug of cream with a dash of whatever passes for coffee around here. It's the lipids that energize, am I right? Tell her what I said, Feldheim."

Feldheim stood rigidly clutching his cap. He translated the major's request to the woman who hurried to fetch a fresh cup. "Will that be all, *Sturmbannführer?*"

"You are not dismissed, if that's your question." He moved to the window and motioned for Feldheim to follow him. "I have some questions for you myself, regarding my recent difficulties with partisans. I'm not familiar with this regiment's protocol in keeping them under control. Is there some sort of execution quota for each sector? The commander tells me he's delegated these responsibilities to his adjutant. Or haven't you bothered?"

Feldheim jerked upright. No one had told him about any executions, though they occurred frequently enough that he could count on one happening somewhere. He'd stopped keeping track long ago because nobody ever asked him for details, or seemed to care. Besides, the commander preferred to pretend they didn't happen, and he could only pretend if no one brought it up.

The woman poured the steaming coffee. She set the cream jug on a nearby table.

"I can ask her for sugar too, *Sturmbannführer*, if you'd like," said Feldheim, thinking that if he could somehow distract or impress the major, Weiss might release him if not pardon him outright. "I think she's stockpiling it in the cellar. No matter what she says about stale madeleines."

Weiss swallowed the coffee the woman handed him in one gulp and chased it with a madeleine. "Hoarding sugar is a capital offense." He turned the cup in his hands as if examining it for cracks. Then he dashed the cup on the floor. Feldheim started.

The woman didn't understand German, but she twitched at the sound of the shattering porcelain. First she looked to Weiss, then to Feldheim. Her lower lip trembled as if this time she might indeed cry. Feldheim stepped toward her, intending to help clear the mess, but Weiss froze him with a noxious glare.

"Beg to report, *Sturmbannführer*. It's only sugar. Not Molotov cocktails."

"The one leads to the other. Either way, she's violated the rules. You have a pistol, Feldheim. Execute her."

Feldheim laughed. He couldn't help it. Of course this was a joke. The woman didn't understand, but she saw him laugh and smiled back, and shrugged as if to say that broken cups could be mended. She emerged from behind the bar with a dustpan and crouched at the major's feet to sweep the shards into a pile.

Weiss drew his pistol while she swept.

Feldheim blinked. The explosion seemed to lacquer that stupid grin to his own face, and in the noiseless vacuum that followed he wondered vaguely if he could sweep her back into her dustpan.

The major's lips pulled taut, forming words around his gritted teeth, the syllables garbled, fading in and out, incomprehensible.

"Beg to report, *Sturmbannführer*," Feldheim heard his own voice say, distant and distorted by static as if piped into the room by some hidden illegal radio. "The sugar. Her sugar. I already got it. From her." Then air rushed from his lungs, sour fluid flooded his mouth. He found himself doubled over the bar, clutching his stomach. The major leaned over him, blocking the light.

The café had grown silent, and Feldheim realized that the phonograph on the side table had reached the end of its last song long ago, yet still the turntable spun with the occasional click, and then he remembered the woman, cocking her head and listening to something that wasn't there. Feldheim couldn't remember the notes now; could no longer hear the music. He pressed his cheek against the countertop, its surface still damp where the woman had swabbed it with her cloth. She'd missed a dusting of sugar crystals, and they loomed as icebergs before his eyes.

"Stand up, *Untersturmführer!*"

Something brushed the back of his head. The major's gun, Feldheim assumed, as he shut his eyes. He couldn't feel his legs, and he clung to the counter to keep from slipping to the floor. What was wrong with him? He wasn't that green. He must have driven past a dozen corpses that morning, but he couldn't call any particular one to mind, just the vague sense of their existence. And though Major Weiss would never believe him, Feldheim had overseen an execution in France—a member of the Resistance who had lobbed a grenade at passing troops from an open window. The colonel had delegated this necessary duty since he himself was needed in the field, and so Feldheim had done his best, offering both the cigarette and the burlap sack to cover the criminal's head, which the man resisted though Feldheim made the guards tie it on anyway. That time he'd been ready for the shot.

"Are you deaf, *Untersturmführer?*" Weiss hissed in his ear. The major must have holstered his weapon because he clamped one arm around Feldheim's neck in a semi-choke hold, entrapping him in the lingering scent of his pipe tobacco. Then the major hoisted him to his feet. Feldheim thought of his father, wreathed in that same cloying smoke, who had long ago gripped his shoulder and hissed at him to stop screaming like a girl and lifted him, leg limp and broken, from the muddy soccer field.

Feldheim breathed through his nose, letting the smell of tobacco muffle his brain like gauze. At last he found his balance and racked his posture back into a soldierly pose just as two Panther crewmen burst in, weapons drawn. Noticing the mess on the floor, they lowered their weapons, faces barren of any shock or emotion.

"We heard a shot, *Sturmbannführer*," said one man in a toneless voice.

The major sent them out again with a sideways chop of his hand. Then he turned back to Feldheim. Pressure from the lengthy silence built inside him, and Feldheim suppressed the urge to clutch his stomach. He had to explain himself somehow, but Weiss would ridicule everything he said. The wrong word would mean a bullet—but not as certainly as disrespectful silence.

"Beg to report, *Sturmbannführer*," said Feldheim slowly. "I think the coffee was bad. But I'll manage," he added, just in case the major concluded that he was a malingerer on top of everything else.

"I can see you are ignorant on many levels," said Weiss, tipping the bowl of madeleines onto the bar. "So I shall try to explain things for your narrow perspective. You have commanded a Panther before, I assume?" he asked doubtfully.

"Yes, *Sturmbannführer*."

"Then you know that as Panther commander I want only to blow the enemy to pieces with my cannon, and crush what's left of him under my treads."

"As a matter of course, *Sturmbannführer*."

Weiss plucked a single madeleine from the bar and crumbled it to dust between his fingers. "But this is only one Panther. By itself it is nothing. I also command a battalion." Now he arranged the remaining madeleines into a row of four. "Four companies. Twenty-two tanks each. Deadly power. Then I see an adjutant whose leader has given him much responsibility but failed to mentor and discipline him. This adjutant is failing his regiment, his entire army, by not taking initiative. This I cannot ignore. This adjutant sees many problems: he sees idle soldiers wasting fuel in a field, he suspects a civilian of withholding rations to our men. Yet he ignores these problems, hoping they will go away. Is this not accurate?"

"It is accurate, *Sturmbannführer*." Feldheim ducked his head, taking care not to let his gaze drop to the floor. He concentrated instead on the mosaic of decorations on the Major's uniform, the only solid focal point in the room.

"But when *I* see a problem, I eradicate it immediately. I even halt the tank. I make my crew sit outside, because I must do it. Do you see the difference?"

Feldheim nodded.

"This adjutant. He himself is a problem. What should I do, *Untersturmführer*? Should I eradicate him, too? Is that fair?"

Feldheim's tongue cleaved to the roof of his mouth. When his voice came at last it rasped, barely audible. "It is fair, *Sturmbannführer*."

"Indeed. But then I have to pull better, braver men off the line to take his place. I will do it if I must. This adjutant was made adjutant for a reason. He showed potential once, as unbelievable to me as that may be. Will he muzzle his weaker instincts and rule them with a will of steel? Can he prove that his loyalty is as pure as his blood?"

Feldheim raised his chin and sucked in another breath. He couldn't avert his eyes from the major's medals. His heartbeat echoed dimly beneath his own depressingly unadorned tunic, then something within him flared like an ember under a bellows, feeding off the vapors of the major's words. A man like Weiss grabbed opportunity by the heels and shook its pockets empty, so Feldheim would do the same.

He stomped and saluted. "My honor is my loyalty!" His voice rang in the long, low room as through a catacomb. This still didn't seem dramatic enough of a gesture to impress Major Weiss, so as Feldheim lowered his outstretched arm he swept it through a shelf of wine glasses on the wall beside him. They crashed to the floor in a sparkling crystal cascade. "This I have sworn until death!"

Major Weiss watched him intently, and Feldheim thought he detected the slightest twitch of approval flicker across his upper lip. "The cabinet with the plates."

Feldheim pivoted on his heel. He wedged his shoulder behind an enormous, oak china hutch. He didn't put enough power into his first push. The hutch rocked forward, its glass doors swinging open against the weight of stacks of china plates that shattered on the floor. Feldheim leveraged it over on his second try. This time the emptied hutch toppled, slow at first, then faster as gravity claimed it until it landed *bom!* facedown like a passed-out drunk.

He noticed the sheen of a pink ribbon on the lumpy pillow hidden in plain sight among a stack of linens behind the bar. He leaned for it, stretched his arm out wide across the bar and snatched it by its unraveled top. As the major watched, he tipped the pillow upside down and shook it over the woman's body. The sugar cloaked her like snow, sopped her up like berry juice, and now Feldheim found he could look at her again, with nothing inside his stomach but a faint, hollow buzz. So much sugar. He hadn't seen so much in years. She was like the proverbial miser who drowned in a pool of golden coins, a criminal like the one he'd blinded with burlap, which meant she'd earned her fate. Otherwise this wouldn't have happened. This he told himself over and over.

"You've wasted enough of my time already," said Weiss. "Let's get out of this hole." He pointed to the window, and the idle infantry beyond. "Now we take care of them. Follow me then go deliver your orders—kill yourself, even. Whatever pleases the regimental commander."

Before he left, Feldheim reached for the last of the madeleines on the bar and put them in his pocket. He didn't care if they were stale. Later, when his stomach unclenched itself, he might put one in his mouth, set it on his tongue, but instead of chewing he would let it dissolve into a spongy wad of flour, butter and sugar, and then he would hold onto the sugar, or the thought of it, and think of how her hands might have rolled the dough between her palms. Maybe he'd detect a hint of salt from her sweat, though he imagined her sweat would have been sweet like the sugar. He might do that. Most likely he'd forget, gulp it down as he drove to the lines, chew and swallow without remembering, and it would be gone, and she gone with it, and he could do nothing more about it.

Weiss preceded Feldheim through the front door, nodding at the tank crew who sat patiently atop the Panther's armored shell, swinging legs and flapping arms for warmth, waiting for their officer. They craned their necks to follow the major and Feldheim as they passed, as if expecting something interesting or profound. Scorch marks blackened the rear armor plates and bullet holes perforated the fenders.

"Start her up again," Weiss ordered the driver, whose head and shoulders protruded from the forward hatch, and pointed at the vacant café. "Send someone to check the cellar, then do what needs to be done. I'll be right back. This will only take a minute." The driver saluted.

Major Weiss slewed on foot across the muddy road as if he were driving his tank, and Feldheim had to jog to keep up with him. The wind tossed tiny ice shards in Feldheim's face. He tilted his visor as far down over his eyes as he could and watched where he placed each boot, navigating the treacherous furrows of frozen mud that had filled with fine granules of snow. Even the snow reminded Feldheim of sugar. His thoughts fizzed away like beer froth from his mind, so he just followed behind the major, keeping his eyes on the back of the black uniform.

In the piebald field across the road, snow crusted the dry tufts of grass and dissolved into brown slush where it had settled into patches of mud. The infantrymen's vehicle tracks striped the snow, a musical staff for their boot-mark notes like an enormous, chaotic orchestral score. Everything else had succumbed to mud. Slabs of it lay in the road where it had dropped from the tank's treads like thick slices of *Lebkuchen*. It spattered the captured jeep, the canvas-topped truck, the open-top *Kübelwagen*, the prisoners. They had muddy knees from kneeling, and muddy hands from being pushed to the ground, or from slipping or falling or begging when they were captured, that they had wiped on their greenish-brown trousers which were already the same color as the mud, and so Feldheim couldn't really tell where the mud ended and their uniforms began. He was glad he didn't have to wear an ugly, mud-colored uniform.

Civilian colors, dark red and blue, flashed among the olive-brown throng of prisoners; two men with hands thrust deep into the pockets of their bulky farmers' coats, most likely interpreters or spies. He couldn't tell if officers were among the prisoners because their helmets were gone, and with them the painted white bars of an officer's rank, though he'd seen some other *Ami* soldiers before—dead ones—who'd smeared mud over their helmets because German snipers liked to pick off the officers first.

The prisoners—he counted ten, maybe twelve—stood in a loose circle, backs to one another, perhaps to keep warm but also to keep their eyes on their captors. Because as Feldheim and Weiss approached, the prisoners facing the road nudged the men next to them, who nudged the men next to them, until all the men in the circle had been nudged. Their heads pivoted to watch the major, then Feldheim, clear the ditch between the road and the field in one leap.

A dozen SS infantrymen looked on, decked out in a variety of issued and captured weapons, along with the necessary coating of mud from the knees down. Three of them leaped from the hood of the idling *Ami* jeep they had captured, where they sat burning precious fuel for the sake of warming their buttocks. One of them hurdled the windscreen to kill the ignition, as if he might avert the barrage of censure homing toward him. The others stood in pairs and chatted with one another, smoking captured cigarettes with glorious abandon, and which must have been plentiful because at the sight of Weiss they flicked half-smoked sticks into the snow without much reluctance. Their banter and shoulder slaps lulled to a nervous murmur.

"Who's in charge here?" bellowed Weiss. "Where's your officer?"

For a few moments none of the SS soldiers spoke. Then one tall enlisted man, an *Oberscharführer* with two captured pistols in his belt and an American M-1 over his shoulder, said, "He's dead."

"So now you're it," pronounced Weiss. "What are your orders?"

"Wait for resupply, refuel, prisoner relief, and head back into the fray. We've been waiting almost two hours. Can't go anywhere like this. With them." He pointed to the prisoners.

"Why the hell did you take prisoners with you?" demanded Weiss.

"We surrounded them. They surrendered."

"And what did you think you were going to do with them?"

"Hand them off at the rear when we get resupplied. We didn't take the wounded. These ones can walk."

Feldheim stood behind the major, off to one side, out of the way. He examined the prisoners with interest while trying to look bored. One of the *Amis*, a tall kid with rounded Anglo features, had a torn sleeve. He'd cut off his unit patch, the stupid ass, as if no one knew the 82nd swarmed the whole damn area. The prisoner noticed Feldheim staring because he stared back with wide eyes slightly magnified behind a round pair of glasses that made him look like a twenty-year-old version of Heinrich Himmler.

Weiss had the SS soldiers line the prisoners up side by side, hands clamped on heads, so he could conduct his own pass and review. Then he went over to the

SS men who had set up a machine gun to guard over the prisoners, its barrel laid over the hood of the *Kübelwagen*.

The infantrymen and their prisoners twitched as one solitary unit. Puffs of steam escaped from between the men's lips, and Feldheim thought he heard a tiny sound like water hissing on a hot stove.

The major whispered into the gunner's ear. A single pop shattered the air, followed by the jagged roar of machine gun fire. The prisoner on the end went down, then the man next to him. The man next to the second prisoner looked like he wanted to run away but he didn't have time to lift a foot because an instant later he was down, too. The other SS men started firing when the *Amis* and the two civilians on the end picked up their feet and started to run. The last man, the one in the blue farmer's coat, slid through the mud onto his chest and lay still.

Feldheim drew his Walther, an instinctual response to the gunfire, but kept his finger braced on the trigger guard. He pointed the muzzle down at the mud until the shooting stopped.

The SS men stood rooted, unwilling to look one another in the eye. They stared at the ground and mumbled loudly to no one in particular.

"One of them creamed my helmet with a snowball and started the whole thing," said one man.

His companion eyed him askance. "You're an idiot to think anyone could make a snowball with this fucking sugar."

"Well there must have been a reason for it."

"Didn't anyone else notice that prisoner holding a gun he had managed to hide in his pocket?" piped up a third soldier with a machine pistol slung on his side. "Maybe it was down his pants. And wasn't he aiming at the lieutenant?"

"Shot while trying to escape," said the first. "That's all."

They nodded back and forth to one another, though a few of the SS men retained slack-jawed expressions as if laboring to convince themselves that they hadn't really just seen that. Done that.

Feldheim guessed he wore the same look on his own face. He adjusted the courier bag on his shoulder and checked that the buckles hadn't come unfastened. A low harmonic moan met his ear, a sound like wind sieving through a shot-up tin can. The gauze in his brain had thickened, and he navigated his thoughts as through a blizzard. At last he gave up and awaited his release from Major Weiss, staring at the field because there was nowhere else to look.

A thunderous explosion sent several of the SS men diving for cover, though they soon wiped the mud from their hands while laughing off jangled nerves. The Panther had fired a shell through the front door of the café. The major shouted orders at the senior infantryman to round up his men, make use of their fucking cigarette tinder to light that blasted building like a solstice bonfire, then haul their asses to the front on foot, and damn all resupply. Feldheim suspected that Weiss had forgotten about him, but as he contemplated slipping away unnoticed, the major spun as if reading his thoughts and jabbed a fist at him.

"*Untersturmführer* Feldheim! Report to me."

Feldheim marched robotically to the major and saluted. He didn't know how else to behave. The unnatural seemed, at that moment, the most natural.

"What did we discuss earlier, *Untersturmführer*?"

"Beg to report, *Sturmbannführer*, that problems must be eradicated."

"Correct. And we have done so. But a duty is not complete unless it is thoroughly checked and verified." He pointed at Feldheim's Walther. "Do you have twelve bullets?"

"More, *Sturmbannführer*."

"Then you can afford to be thorough. When you have completed this task, you are dismissed."

So Feldheim drew his loaded pistol, much heavier than he remembered, and walked through the field while the major tracked his progress by counting off the shots. When Heinrich Himmler looked up and mouthed some indistinct English word, Feldheim aimed for the strip of metal where the eyeglasses bridged the man's nose. His bare finger clung white and frozen to the trigger. He closed his eyes and pulled.

Sometime later Feldheim stood before the café, *Hotel des Ardennes*, his cold, bare fingers stiffened into claws.

Whirling flakes of ash brushed his face and settled in the snow around his feet in tiny black craters. He pressed his eyelids together until stars exploded in his field of view. In his mind he wound the scene in reverse like a spool of film, retracting his own footprints from the churned and ruddy snow. The Walther's kickback jerked his arm. It swallowed bullets back into the chamber as he fired in mid-blink. A tangle of olive-drab limbs slurred backwards through the snow, and black smoke wound down into the café's bare sockets as if the smashed-out windows sucked it in.

No. He'd missed something. Something wasn't right. He felt in his pocket for his gloves and pulled out a crumbled madeleine instead. He chewed it and tried to remember as burnt wood shavings filled his mouth. Smoke dwindled to a single curl and disappeared. Glass fragments leapt from the snow, crystallizing into windowpanes like ice. A woman cocked her head, listening for her sleeping children to wake. He could see her face framed there now by lace curtains, her eyes wide and dull behind the glass as if she stared up at him through a frozen pond, already a corpse. The phonograph inhaled unearthly strains of a melody played in reverse.

The Rites of Summer

Rachael Warecki

Antioch University Los Angeles, Low Residency MFA

The wedding of Darren Corner and Katie Granados had been advertised as an outdoor affair, but in reality the ceremony took place under a tent, a monstrosity that must have looked white to outsiders, but showed only its gray underbelly to those of us who'd been selected as honored guests. There were glimpses of the outside, every now and then when something important happened—the bridesmaids' entrance, the ring-bearers, the bride herself bouncing down the aisle—but these glimpses only frustrated me; they crept around my senses like echoing whispers, reminding me of what could have been, what could have been.

I didn't know anyone else at this wedding, outside of the bride and groom, and they were too busy enacting their ritual to stand at my side in the audience and swelter along with their nearest and dearest. There was no one to whom I could point out the elegant Southern gentleman in the boater hat, whose sweat stains threatened the integrity of his three-piece cream-colored suit. The woman next to me, a sad lonely lump of a person, had eyes and ovaries only for the flower girls; I could hardly lean over and tell her that I thought they looked slightly too old for their role in these shenanigans, like chicks halfway to hens, their eyes searching for escape routes, their hands fighting the urge to loosen their lace collars and let slivers of cool air slide between their breasts like lovers' fingers. The best thing about being the bride and groom, I decided, was their possession of space: no one pressed too closely against that white dress, no one clung to those tuxedo tails; even the reverend—or the priest or the pastor, I've never been good with denominational nomenclature—hovered from a respectful distance. It was a wedding gift, this distance, a recognition that these were the last instants in which the bride and groom could enjoy their individual, personal, single space before cleaving to each other as the mono-entity man and wife. I've reveled in that particular kind of space for half a decade, darting from Ohio to Portland to Madrid to California whenever something or someone tried to make me compromise, and I wondered if Darren and Katie, running toward this head-on collision that would fuse them together forever, realized the freedom they were giving up.

I had expected the wedding to be more of a mess, considering the parties involved, and the beauty of the ceremony—the delicacy of the bride's mother, the stoic silence of the groom's family, the doves released into the air as the couple took their vows—settled beneath my ribs like a disappointing meal at a five-star restaurant. This was Texas, after all, a state to which I'd never been and which often seems a lot farther from California than it actually is. I had dipped into my savings for these plane tickets, I had scrounged extra writing gigs for months in order to afford my motel room, and I'd expected some kind of payoff, some kind of circus in which everything became larger than life, an event that would serve as a well to which I could return again and again for stories that would capture the decay of the American Dream. But Darren had remained his dull, compliant self, right down to the way in which his speckling of white hairs complemented the color of his bride's dress, and Katie had reined in her exuberance until it shone only for her husband; her guests, starving for it, hadn't even gotten one of her smiles. Even the doves, who had hinted at the possibility of a literal shit-show when released into the tent, followed their cue to the letter, making their way from the altar to the tent opening without so much as a dropping.

The reception was outdoors. We guests, after applauding the married couple's first kiss, followed the doves, but one glance at the round, white tables, sunken lopsidedly into the grass like matrimonial land mines, reminded me that I had no idea where I was supposed to sit. I paused. I thought, briefly, that I didn't want to be rude, I didn't want to upset Darren and Katie on their wedding day by sitting in some maiden aunt's place of honor, but then I remembered that Darren and Katie wouldn't notice my error, hadn't given any sign yet that they'd noticed my presence at all, and that even if I made some offensive mistake, the ceremony would then divorce itself from its script and roll merrily into the kind of spontaneous drama that I'd hoped to see when I'd purchased my plane tickets. I chose the first available chair.

"Are you a friend of the bride's or a friend of the groom's?" It was the Southern gentleman I'd seen during the wedding. Now that we were out in the open, his three-piece suit seemed to breathe more easily, like an asthmatic recovering from an attack.

"Both," I said.

"Really." He removed a pair of spectacles from one of his pockets and scrutinized me; when he sat down, I thought I heard his suit exhale. "Because I'm Darren's uncle, and I don't recall ever meeting you before, Miss."

"I'm not sure if you could really call me a friend," I said. "I'm from California. I only met Darren and Katie last summer."

As I said their names, we both turned to find them. In a break with tradition—I'd guess it was Katie's doing—the couple had decided to cut the cake first, and Katie was standing, slice in hand, ready to redecorate Darren's face. There was something about Katie that had always reminded me of a dessert. Maybe it was her roundness, a super-voluptuousness that had eluded my stick-thin frame, a sense that she was always about to burst out of her clothes, which clung to her in a combination of too-tight and too-loose, an idea that her natural, most comfortable state was in the nude. Or maybe it was her eagerness; her ability to suggest with just a look in your direction that she was ready and willing for whatever adventure you might come up with. There was an irresistible lightness to her, like angel food cake, and it was easy to see why, during that week last summer when I'd known her best, she'd brought a different man home every night. And yet Darren was the man she'd ended up with, a man who'd been born and raised in South Carolina and had never left, except for the five years he'd spent in New Orleans before and after Hurricane Katrina. His stodginess had etched itself into his bones, and every time he looked at Katie, he seemed surprised that he and his middle age had managed to catch this twenty-something miracle of a girl.

Katie aimed her slice at Darren's face and the icing exploded, covering his nose and mouth until only his eyes were left, and I remembered the night when he and Katie had met, when he'd talked about New Orleans and his eyes had gone sad, and I thought maybe that was what Katie had seen in him after all.

The Southern gentleman turned back to me. "You said you met them last summer. Was that before or after their engagement?"

"Before," I said. "But not that long before. In fact, I brought them together."

There had been two of us under thirty at the writers' conference in Iowa, a fact that had bothered Katie a lot more than it had bothered me. We'd met at the opening dinner and she'd shaken her head, scanning the other attendees with a heightened sense of disbelief. "There are no fuckable guys here," she said. "In fact, you and I are the only fuckable girls. I bet everyone else here is married." She clearly meant it as an opening, a chance to commiserate, but I was relieved: no chance, then, that someone would read my writing and try to sneak into my heart. I could leave Iowa as free as I had arrived, with nothing more solid than friendships trailing in my wake. I already knew that friendships could be maintained at any distance, and besides, I was there for a specific purpose. There was a novel, half of a non-starter that I was determined to finish, about my time in Madrid. I didn't know Katie's purpose, yet; as far as I could tell on that first night, she was a poet who specialized in haikus, a memoirist bored by her own childhood, a flash-fiction devotee, a novelist who'd abandoned a dozen unfinished manuscripts. She didn't have a relationship with writing; she had one-night stands.

We'd gone about our own business that week, meeting at a coffee shop in the mornings, she to tell me about her nightly conquests and me to fret over my novel. I'm not sure why she and Darren didn't meet until that last night, because

I'd become close with Darren and his manuscript, a dystopia set in a future New Orleans that was struggling to survive a series of man-made and natural disasters. But Katie had seemed content with her line of college town boys, and so I'd never pulled her into the writing aspect of the conference, not until that last night when the next day meant goodbye and I'd wanted them both with me—that bubbly, careless girl, and the man whose homesickness I couldn't comprehend.

We'd met at a bar, which was close and smoky and tucked between two other close, smoky places. The wooden floor was inlaid with silver dollars and framed bullets decorated the wall; it was the type of bar that doesn't invite trouble, but doesn't discourage it, either. Darren had brought along another woman from the conference, a black-haired Frenchwoman named Jeannine whose every movement was robust, and we'd squeezed into a booth, Jeannine and I on one side and Darren and Katie on the other, as if the conclusion had been foregone before any of us had realized it.

We ordered beers and had been drinking for maybe a half-hour, at the slow, easy pace of people enjoying each other's company, when a boy slid into the booth next to me, squishing my hips between his and Jeannine's. "Excuse me," I said, but he didn't look at me; his eyes were on Katie, and the hot, clear glass of ownership had slid over them: one of Katie's townie conquests, I guessed, who hadn't realized that he was one of a string. His glasses perched on florid cheeks; his tongue darted against his lips.

"Come on, Katie," he said. "Let's get out of here."

"I don't think so," Katie said.

"We're enjoying ourselves," Jeannine added, from my other side. Her voice floated across my shoulders, as cool and easy as a shower, but it did nothing to calm the boy.

"Come on, Katie," he repeated. "There's no one here. This place is dead. Let's go somewhere fun."

I was relieved when Katie shook her head. I itched between the two bodies packed against me; I felt like gum stuck to the underside of desk, but the idea of unsandwiching myself from one side of the boy made me wary. Jeannine tried again: "If Katie wants to spend time with you, she'll come find you later, okay?" Darren nodded in time with the rhythms of her speech. Even Darren, whose workshop critiques were most noteworthy for their uncertainty, their fishy flip-flopping, knew that he wanted this boy gone.

The boy's eyes turned glassier, his cheeks redder. "Did you guys all get your periods at the same time?" he asked, his gaze passing over Darren like the angel of death, removing him from the conversation as quickly as those Egyptian boys for whom blood had not been an option. "You're behaving like bitches. PMS-y bitches." He pointed a finger at each of us in turn, even Darren. "You're a bitch," he said to Katie. "*You're* a bitch"—to Jeannine, and then to me—"*you're* a bitch…"

I slapped him.

The boy blinked and adjusted his glasses, which had come askew from the force of my hand. "Oh, come on. That wasn't even hard."

I slapped him again and this time my palm was fresh against his left cheek, for symmetry. A glass of ice water, hidden among our beer steins, tipped and spilled across the table.

"Come on!" The boy's glasses had come off and his voice had reached a strange, high pitch; his sanity, like the ice cubes, seemed to be melting, and I wondered if he knew how to start a conversation with any other phrase but *come on*. "Slap me again! You know you want to! Slap me again!"

But Jeannine had pulled me into a maternal headlock and Darren, bounding into action, surprised me out of my anger. The three of us watched as Darren grabbed the boy's arm, yanked him out of the booth, and escorted him to the door. He returned five minutes later and slid into his seat as if he'd spent his entire adulthood slinging South Carolina boys out into summer nights.

"What?" Darren said. "It wasn't right, the way he was talking to you ladies." He turned to Katie. "Especially not to you," he said, and her hand slid gratefully over his.

The foregone conclusion had begun, right before my eyes, and the next morning, when Katie and I had met one last time at the coffee shop, her eyes had shone with the kind of victory I associated with religious converts and cult leaders. "I'm engaged," she'd confided, and she'd told me about what happened after Jeannine and I had peeled ourselves from that close, smoky bar and returned to our hotel rooms. The moonlight walk that had led to the banks of the Iowa River. The nightlong conversation that had led to a mutual declaration of love and admiration, followed by a proposal. The furious lovemaking that had taken place at the riverside, Katie's clothes removed—her body following through on that promise—so that the long, smooth reeds had tickled her skin as she'd rolled and gasped and given the rest of her life to a Southern gentleman. I didn't believe her until Darren arrived, removed a piece of string from his pocket, and tied it around the ring finger of her left hand; the sadness in his eyes lifted, slightly.

They had known each other for less than twelve hours.

I was glad to leave Iowa that afternoon. The engagement had rubbed something raw just below my skin, reminding me of all the compromises I had worked so hard to avoid, and I escaped imagining that had I stayed, their monogamy might have become contagious, moving through the conference attendees as swiftly and lethally as Ebola—but not before I'd taken my own walk down by the riverside, looking for the impressions in the grass that would confirm the fairy tale I'd just heard. And I found them: two dips where the reeds had been flattened, looking as if a pair of birds had nested there before suddenly deciding to take flight.

I didn't tell that story to the Southern gentleman next to me—whatever Katie and Darren had told their families about their engagement was between them, and I wondered who'd come up with it, Katie and her flights of haiku or Darren and his book-length dedication—and besides, the story seemed sad now, out of place among this carefully orchestrated ceremony where all the attendees seemed to have finished whatever they'd started in their own long-ago youths.

"And what about you?" the gentleman asked. Katie and Darren had finished the cake and moved to the dance floor, where the band had started playing something stately and appropriate, the horns low and somber as if they'd been reined in when all they really wanted was to gallop up and down the scales, kicking and bucking and free. "A pretty girl like you, you're probably planning your own wedding."

"No," I said. "It's different out in California." I didn't add that, for me, it had also been different out in Portland and in Ohio and in Madrid.

The gentleman smiled. "I think you're being dishonest with me, Miss. Every young woman has her plans, even if she doesn't have the man to go along with them."

"Fine. To honesty." I raised my water glass. "When I get married, I don't want any of this." Through the glass, I watched Katie and Darren move in slow, concentric circles, barely dancing at all, their steps warped by my ice cubes. I imagined all the household surfaces that would suffer the marks of their marital non-movement: the sofa cushion where Katie would sit her ever-widening hips; the barstool where Darren would rest each evening, for longer and longer periods, as he finished a beer before his return home; the invisible line down the middle of their bed that they'd eventually stop crossing, marking their territories, his and hers. "When I get married, I want to dance the jitterbug."

On the walk back to my motel, down the street from the park where the wedding had taken place, I watched the sun set and imagined Katie and Darren growing old together. I imagined Darren publishing his novel and Katie, shining with his achievement, settle down to one literary form. The thought of her spending the rest of her life devoted to memoir or to poetry or to fiction—the idea of her giving up even these flings—tugged at me more than the wedding itself had done, followed me into my bed like an unwanted lover, until, at two in the morning, I flung off my covers and went to the window.

There was a full moon that night, and what's more, there was a river, slipping away behind the hotel as if it didn't want to call attention to itself, as if it was planning its escape. As I watched the light reflect and refract off the river's surface, the water refusing even that relationship, I saw movement along the riverbanks: two shapes, their outlines uncertain in the darkness. They could have been anything, those shapes. Years later, when writing the story of Darren and Katie's wedding, perhaps I would leave this part out, dismiss it as a trick of the moonlight or as one of the thousand and one ways in which animals have learned to live among humans. But standing there, watching the shapes nestle and shuffle and come together and break apart, I saw two people making love, two birds about to take flight.

The Feast of All Souls

Monica Macansantos

The Michener Center for Writers, University of Texas, MFA

I clutched a pair of flesh-colored candles as I followed my mother through the crowd. At nine in the morning the Baguio Cemetery was awash in sunlight and the smell of steamed corn, roasted peanuts, car exhaust, and newly washed hair gave the air a thick and confusing aroma. We had a quick, simple breakfast, of *pan de sal* and butter at dawn before taking a jeepney to the cemetery, where the smell of food made my stomach growl. But my mother was too determined to find what she was looking for, and if I asked her for money she probably wouldn't hear my voice above the din.

A man in a faded brown cap thrust a stick broom in my mother's face. "Ma'am, you need cleaners? We can clean your tomb for you," he said.

My mother stopped. "How much?" she asked.

"One hundred pesos."

My mother stepped back in surprise, and I followed her when she skirted past him. "Too expensive," she said, brushing him away.

The man caught up with my mother. "What about eighty pesos?" he asked.

"Sixty."

One could always tell by the sound of her voice that she knew what she wanted.

"Take pity on me Ma'am, I have children to feed."

A short, sunburned woman with a scar on her cheek approached us. "Ma'am, I can clean your tomb for sixty pesos."

A man in paint-stained overalls spotted us and hurried to my mother. He held a can of paint in my mother's face and said, "Maybe your tomb needs a paint job, too. I can do it for fifty pesos."

"*Sige, sige,*" my mother said, squinting in the sunlight as she beckoned them to follow.

My mother took my hand as we entered a narrow concrete passageway at the side of the cemetery's main plaza. Rocks, twigs, and crushed flowers littered our path. The passageway opened to reveal a hill sloping downwards. Whitewashed tombs were crammed into every inch of space. They looked like tiny, unopened boxes, and I could imagine myself fitting my shoes into them. Concrete cherubs sat on the tombs, eyes downcast, hands clasped.

My mother stepped on one that read *Baby Michael Flores, R.I.P.* "Watch your step" she said, and squeezed my hand.

We tried not to step on the boxes as we made our way downhill. "When your dad and I came here last year we were able to find the spot where your cousin is entombed. It's always hard for me to find. The adults are taking over and edging out the children." I nearly tripped on an overturned tomb with a decapitated cherub. Nearby, two boys and a woman stood on a small, grimy box, praying before a larger, freshly painted box that rose to their waists. Another family sat in a circle on top of a marble grave, eating *longganisa* and rice from paper plates.

Farther down the hill, a group of dark-skinned men in working clothes stood on a white tomb at the foot of a pine tree, hauling away a pile of leaves and branches and dropping them into a wide, rectangular hole in the earth. "If my memory serves me right, it's right in front of that tree," she said. When her gaze settled on the group of men, she dropped my hand. "Wait!" she yelled. "What do you think you're doing?"

She scrambled down the hill and I held my breath, hoping she wouldn't slip and fall. The woman with a scar on her cheek clicked her tongue and said, "*Naku*, Ma'am is angry."

"That's my niece's grave you're turning into a dump!" my mother hollered. My ears burned as people turned to look at her.

A gray-haired mustached man scratched his head. "Sorry, *ha* Ma'am. We were hired to clean this tomb. *Uy*," he hissed at his companions, waving a hand at them, "clean up your mess."

One of the younger workers jumped into the hole. "But where do we throw these?"

"Anywhere," the tall man answered, waving a hand at the sea of white boxes on the hillside.

This was the first time my mother brought me to the cemetery to visit my cousin Erika on the Feast of All Souls. She and my father had gone the year before to pay their respects, but this year I was taking my father's place. "Shouldn't you tell *Manang* Carmen to visit her own daughter? She comes to Baguio all the time," he said when my mother announced a week before our visit that the Feast of All Souls was fast approaching. We were having breakfast, and my father tossed his newspaper aside after my mother spoke.

"You know how *Manang* Carmen is. She can't be talked into doing something she doesn't want to do," she said, stirring her coffee.

I poured a heart on my pancake with a spoon from the honey bottle my mother handed to me. I drew hearts everywhere: on my notebook pages, in the sketchbooks my father bought me for my birthday, in my diary, on my food. I especially liked to do it when I was bored, like when grownups talked to each other without talking to me. When I sensed my mother was looking at me, I closed the lid of the honey bottle and swung my legs under the table.

"Seems like your father doesn't want to come with me to visit your cousin's grave. Do you want to keep me company instead?" my mother asked.

"So now Ina's officially part of the family tradition," my father grumbled.

"I can come with you, Ma." I knew this was what my mother wanted me to say, and a smile broke on her face. I wondered what I was supposed to do when I went with her, and why she needed me to be there. I didn't know how to behave in a cemetery, especially one that had babies in it.

"It's Erika Gallardo. Born June 1, 1971, died June 3, 1971," my mother told the painter after he had lowered himself into the pit. She died ten years before I was born, and I only know her from the photos of her burial tucked into the pages of our family album. In one picture, a group of adults and children surround a tiny wooden coffin. My Tita Carmen stands at the center of the group, her face half-hidden beneath a veil of black lace, while my mother, dressed in bell-bottoms and a black buttoned-up sweater, stands beside her. This was before my mother was married, and she was still slim and sexy because she was yet to have me. I am a ghost in this picture, a child waiting to be born. They're in the middle of a grassy field. There weren't as many dead babies back then.

I sometimes wonder whether Erika and I would've been friends had she lived. She would've been a grown woman by this time, perhaps as pretty and stylish as her mother. Maybe she would've been fun to be with, or maybe she would've been like her brothers who never spoke to me whenever they came to Baguio with my Tita in the summertime. I had always wanted a big sister, but she was just a tiny baby my mother visited every year. I wondered if she even knew us, and whether she was just waiting for her mother to visit her instead.

After Erika's death, Tito Mar was offered a job in Manila and Tita Carmen and their children followed him. Manila was good to Tita Carmen, my mother said. The women she played *mahjong* with didn't know she was the daughter of a jeepney driver, nor did they know she had a child named Erika.

Now the painter raised his head. "Wait *lang* Ma'am. I have to clean it first." He opened his bag of tools, pulled out a rusty pair of scissors, and proceeded to scrape off bits of caked mud and moss from the tomb's surface. If my mother wanted me to do something, I could have drawn a heart on Erika's tomb with the man's paints, but I didn't ask. I think she just wanted company.

We sat at the edge of a stonewashed tomb that overlooked the pit, facing the group of men my mother yelled at who were now whitewashing the cleared tomb. Whenever the man in the pit stood his head brushed my feet, and it would've been easy for me to give his head a painful bump with my baby-blue sandals. Erika's tomb wasn't originally in a pit. Over the years, people had piled soil around it and placed their relatives' tombs on top of these heaps. The tomb of *Arturo Borromeo, R.I.P.* had a corrugated iron roof and the relatives had not arrived yet, so we sat under it for shade.

Smoke rose from a pile of burning garbage at the top of the hill. The wind blew the smoke in our faces, and my mother tied a handkerchief around my nose and mouth. At the bottom of the hill the ground rose again, and at the edge of the cemetery a patch of sunflowers swayed in the breeze. It was the first day of November and a chill was beginning to set in. I wondered whether Erika ever got scared or lonely, or if she even remembered her mother. When my mother tucked me into bed the night before, she spread a comforter over my thick Ilocano blanket and pulled socks onto my feet, and a sudden loneliness swept over me when she switched off the lights and closed my door.

My Tita Carmen would make frequent business trips to Baguio and was a regular guest in our household. I looked forward to her visits because of the gifts she'd bring me: teddy bears, faux-gold jewelry, beaded hair scrunchies, and on one occasion, a Barbie doll. My mother chided her for spoiling me, upon which she'd laugh and retort, "Your daughter will only be young once!" Sometimes I imagined Erika staring down at us from heaven, wishing she could be mean to me.

My parents would pick my Tita Carmen up at the bus station in the evening, and when a clicking of heels echoed across our pinewood-paneled house I'd rush to the living room and there she'd be, smiling brightly, jingling with gold jewelry. She'd bend down, take me in her arms, and press a powdery cheek against mine.

"And how is my little *pamangkin*? What grade are you in *na ba*?" she would always ask, no matter how many times I had answered these questions before.

My mother would trail behind her, clad in her usual black slacks and denim jacket, while my father would hobble into the living room carrying my Tita's brown Louis Vuitton suitcases.

"You know *naman* that I was in Hong Kong last week to do some shopping for my business," she said the last time she visited. "I bought early Christmas gifts for you and *na rin*. You have to be ready for 1992 as early as now. As for me, I'm more than ready to get rid of the year of volcanic eruptions and massacres." She unzipped one of her suitcases, rummaged through the odds and ends inside, and fished out a potbellied Buddha. "I noticed that you don't have any of these in your house so I got one for you. Leave it in your living room and it will attract luck."

"Do you have one in your office?" my father asked, amused.

"Of course. It's good for business," Tita Carmen said. She sauntered across the floorboards and placed the Buddha on top of our upright piano. Its fat arms were raised in glee, and I wondered whether the sad-faced Mama Mary standing beside it took offense.

Over dinner Tita Carmen talked about her Chinese herbal medicine business, Tito Mar's law practice, and my cousins Nico and Raul, whom my parents called rich spoiled brats behind my Tita's back. "They're both on the San Agustin High basketball team right now, can you imagine that? I never imagined them growing up so fast. One of their teammates is the son of Congressman Webb, and there's another boy on their team who's the son of a senator," she said, slicing her steak.

"That's good. They can make the right connections in case they want to enter politics," my father said, cupping his glass of wine.

"Hay *naku*, politics is so messy. It's good enough to know some people up there in case one gets into trouble."

Tita Carmen brought out her gifts later that night. There was a set of three wooden monkeys that were supposed to attract luck, a Chinese silk pajama set for me, a silk tie and a bottle of Tiger balm for my father, incense sticks for the living room, and a blood-red Cheong Sam for my mother. "Good heavens, where on earth will I wear this?" my mother cried as she lifted the Cheong Sam from its box.

"In the office, while teaching. Why not?" Tita Carmen said.

"*Manang*, do you want me to look like Mother Lily? My students would laugh at me if I wore this."

"Why, can't you be a *Donya* in the classroom? It's better for them to know who's the boss," Tita Carmen said, raising a penciled eyebrow. "Besides, red is a lucky color. The Chinese wear it to attract good fortune and ward off evil spirits."

"I guess we need all the luck we can get," my mother said, folding the Cheong Sam and putting it back in its box.

A fog descended on the valley as I dug into the cup of hot *taho* my mother bought from a wandering vendor. We were waiting for the paint on Erika's tomb to dry. Meanwhile, the painter had disappeared, perhaps to look for another customer, another tomb. "When are we going home?" I asked, spooning out a mixture of dark syrup and soft, white bean curd.

My mother gazed into the fog. "After the man returns and finishes the lettering. *Naku*, will the paint ever dry in this weather?"

"Ma, why didn't Tita Carmen come with us to visit Erika?"

"Your Tita Carmen is a busy lady. She has to attend to her business in Manila and can't stay long whenever she's here," my mother said. "Besides, can you imagine her walking down this hill in her high-heeled shoes?"

The image of Tita Carmen tripping on a tomb and rolling downhill made me burst into laughter. My mother smiled, relieved perhaps that she could still make me laugh.

"Be careful, child. You might fall." As she said this, her smile faded, and she put her arm around my waist.

Fog was shrouding everything now. The grove of pine trees in the distance, the tombs that surrounded us, the iron poles that supported our roof, the families who combed the hill clutching flowers and candles as they searched for the tombs of their departed. Even my mother's wispy hair seemed to be fading into the mist, and for a split second I imagined her vanishing into the whiteness.

Tita Carmen would always bring a certain lightheartedness into our home, and whenever it was time for her to leave it seemed as though her good humor would leave our home as well. Maybe this was because my parents had no one else to laugh at when she was gone. Or maybe we had more things to talk about whenever she was around. Over dinner she'd share stories of her clients and the people she called her "marketers" whom she'd meet whenever she was in town. There was the student who sold skin-whitening cream to her classmates to finance her college education, the housewife whose husband became a Muslim and took a second wife after going to Saudi Arabia to work as a mechanic, the old tomboy who lived alone and couldn't bend her joints unless she smeared Tiger balm on them, the elderly priest who drank seven-herbs tea and could now lift weights and jog around Burnham Lake. Every story she told had a happy ending, and it seemed as though every problem could be solved with the help of her merchandise.

Tita Carmen dined with us the night before she returned to Manila, and as my mother served dessert Tita Carmen said, "Vicky, you could be one of my marketers too. Just start small and who knows, maybe you could make enough to buy a new car for Eddie."

My mother set a bowl of sweet rice cakes before my Tita. "You know that I'm not good at selling things," my mother said.

"All you have to do is to smile more often."

My mother giggled. "Oh *Manang*, you know how hard it is for me to smile without a reason."

"Just think of your future prosperity whenever you make a sale. That's a good enough reason." Tita Carmen beamed.

My mother returned to her seat. "Not everyone's like you, *Manang*."

"Shit," my mother muttered under her breath as she relit the candles on the edge of Erika's tomb. The fog had lifted, the whitewash had dried, and the lettering was finished, but a smart November wind was blowing, descending into the pit where my mother stood. She'd cup her hand around a freshly lit flame but the wind had a way of sneaking through her fingers and extinguishing whatever she managed to ignite.

I sat at the edge of Arturo Borromeo's tomb and tapped my empty plastic *taho* cup with my spoon. "Ma, I'm hungry," I called down to her.

"But you just had *taho*."

"I want corn now."

"Ina, don't be a brat."

She finally managed to keep two candles burning and kept her hands spread over the flames as she stood up. When the wind still hadn't blown them out she made the sign of the cross, clasped her hands, and bowed her head. I stopped swinging my legs and fixed my eyes on the cherub sitting on Erika's tomb, wondering if it had been preparing all along to mirror my mother's position.

Men in working clothes combed the hill as my mother prayed, eyeing the unpainted tombs and the families who kept searching. A frail, gray-haired man descended the hill leaning on a wooden cane for support, nodding at what he saw. When he passed the pit where my mother stood he stopped and looked down. He raised an eyebrow when he spotted her, as though he never expected to find any living thing where she stood. My mother opened her eyes and made the sign of the cross, and when she looked up she saw him.

"I wouldn't expect anyone to be visiting a tomb this old and hidden," he said.

My mother narrowed her eyes. "Who are you?"

"I'm the caretaker of this cemetery. I've been working here for years and I've seen some of these babies abandoned for good. But this one always has a fresh coat of paint after the Feast of All Souls."

"We come here every year."

He looked at me, smiled, and asked, "Are you visiting your brother or sister?"

"She's my cousin."

"And where are the parents?"

"They're in Manila. I'm the one who visits now," my mother said.

The old man leaned on his cane as he gazed down the hill. "I always think that people will build a tomb over your niece, but thankfully only weeds cover her."

"That's why I come. When they see a clean tomb with a fresh coat of paint, they'll think twice." My mother sighed and looked at me. "I can't just leave her here."

The man winked at me and walked away, and my mother bowed her head to finish praying.

For a moment I was ashamed of how I had behaved. I sat still, out of respect, the way my mother wanted me to. When I had the urge to move I imagined myself drawing hearts on the fresh white walls. I even imagined drawing hearts on my mother, crouched on the floor of the tomb praying like a cherub.

After a while, when the man was far away my mother got up. As she struggled out of the pit she raised her hand, and I took it even though I was afraid I would fall in.

We held hands as we made our way up the hill. I wondered whether the babies inside the tombs got mad when we stepped on them, but where else would we steady our feet? We didn't do it on purpose. They were just in our way.

"God, I hope I can find that tomb next year," my mother said, scowling.

"I'll help you find it, Ma," I said.

She stopped in her tracks and turned to look at me. Her shock seemed to wash away the scowl on her face, and her eyes softened. "Would you do that for me?" she asked.

"Yeah."

Children in rags tripped down the hill, their slippers slapping against concrete. Some had already made it to the bottom of the valley and were picking melted candles from abandoned tombs, pressing them together to form balls of wax they would later sell.

My mother squeezed my hand and said, "I'll get you ice cream before we go home." I let her lead the way.

Sapere Aude

Brendan Park

UC Irvine, MFA

She arrived at the dissection holding a sketchbook and pen rather than an anatomy manual and scalpel. I never had an artist attend one of my dissections, and had she not been so beautiful, perhaps I would have protested the fact that she didn't ask my permission to sit in. I looked at her frequently during the lesson but never once saw her look back at me. Even after the other students left, she remained seated beside an operating table, staring at the blue-white face of the cadaver she was drawing. I told her she was welcome to finish whatever she was working on, but that it would have to be the last sketch, as I needed to lock up.

That evening she ordered Cornish hen. She cleaved muscle from bone with surgical precision, taking rapid, dainty bites, in a manner common to aristocrats and certain birds. She told me that depicting the human form was her only calling in life and that she was born to privilege but had shunned it. She discussed dropping out of school, how she embraced the life of a bohemian and refused her family's money. I told her about the sort of surgery I performed, that it was isolating, and that I taught the anatomy class on a purely volunteer basis as a way to maintain a certain level of interaction with people. When she undid her black braid I took a moment to glance over my wine glass and admire her large green eyes, and pale, sculpted face.

She did not come home with me that night. It remained unspoken, but was clear enough, that each of us wanted to savor the tension a little longer. I paid the cab driver, shut the door behind her, and saw my reflection overlap with hers as the car drove down the wet asphalt.

I decided to walk back to my apartment, but even after thirty minutes and twenty flights of stairs, I was still full of energy. I collected the garbage in my office, bathroom, bedroom, and kitchen and consolidated it all into a single monstrous load, which I took the insufficient precaution of double bagging. I skipped the elevator and again opted for the stairs, bounding down each flight, excited by the thought of rearranging my flat. There was a large alcove with windows ideally situated for sunlight, and already my mind had set up an easel and stool for her there.

The air felt good on my skin as I walked into the alley. Several times I tried to pry open the dumpster lid with one hand while hefting the trash with the other, but the bag was too heavy. I set it down and tried throwing the lid back with both hands, only to have it chomp back down on my fingers. Reluctantly I wedged myself between two dumpsters and opened the lid from the side. I walked back to the front, hefted the bag with both hands, and, just before hurling it into the maw, glimpsed an oddly spaced pair of golden eyes staring out from inside the blackness. My heart stopped and I balked, causing the bag to catch the edge of the dumpster and hang there like a body torn down the side, leaking entrails of paper and vegetable matter.

As I climbed the stairs I kept replaying the image of those eyes in my mind, becoming progressively more agitated with each step. Back in my apartment I reasoned that it must have been a raccoon or stray animal, yet I couldn't match the color and size of those eyes, or their intelligent manner of looking at me, with any animal I had seen before. Of course there are a million things that can alter and trick a man's perception, not least of which is the dark. This thought eventually consoled me and freed my mind to move on to other anxieties. Like what sorts of revealing items, for instance, had been in the enormous bag of trash that I had so carelessly thrown away? With dread I imagined all the possible secrets of my life spilling from the bag and blowing about the streets, vulnerable to the judgment of on-looking eyes. When at last I fell asleep, I dreamed that, while in the midst of giving a lecture, my hand detached from my body and inched away from me. I maintained my composure at the lectern and plodded on mechanically through my talking points but behind me I could hear chalk scratching against the blackboard. I continued talking as though nothing were happening, as though the writing would not exist if I didn't acknowledge it, but from my students' faces I inferred that my hand had written something awful, something that deeply undermined everything I had come to say.

"Henry & Sophia Mann." There we were together, bound in name and print in handsome font along the spine of the book that I had written and she had illustrated. It was only a brief spasm of vanity that made me hesitate about including her name on the book, and really, when I remembered all the others I tried to collaborate with on the project—their crude, overexposed photographs, or their overly stratified drawings that looked like cross sections from geology textbooks—I knew that I couldn't have made a better book with anyone else in the world. Beyond its scientific significance and beyond the clarifying nature of the depictions, the book was something that transcended both of us, a work of art unto itself. I had the book I wanted, I had the wife I wanted, and the easel was in the alcove exactly where I had imagined it would be only a few years before.

On the evening before the release we arranged our apartment into a gallery featuring Sophia's original artwork, each canvas illuminated in soft light and labeled with descriptive placards. I felt vaguely (absurdly) slighted by the fact that Sophia's work should be so much more conspicuous than my own, but then that's just the nature of such an event. Who in their right mind wants to read medical text while drinking champagne? My ego was soothed by the good-natured envy of our peers; overheard snippets between the artists and doctors in attendance suggesting that Sophia and I represented the perfect union of artistic and analytical; that the book was our metaphor, or we were its.

After everyone left Sophia and I gathered the dishes scattered throughout the apartment and scraped bits of leftover food and napkins into the garbage. I hoisted the bags over my shoulder and headed to the alley, leaving Sophia to start on the dishes.

Something odd brushed against the back of my hand while I was stuffing the trash into the dumpster. At first I thought it was merely another trash bag, but a second later I knew what I had just experienced was the unmistakable sensation of skin against skin. It was not a pelt, nothing that could be mistaken for a raccoon or cat, and the shape was not conventionally mammalian. It was something akin to human skin, but a few degrees warmer and utterly glabrous. As had happened on the occasion several years before, I bolted.

Sophia noticed the shortness of my breath when I rejoined her in the kitchen. "Not wise to climb so many stairs after heavy drinking," she said, not unkindly. "There's an elevator in this building, you know."

"It's nothing," I said. She continued washing dishes and I stood behind her with my arms around her waist, resting my chin on her shoulder. "There's a monster living in our dumpster, is all."

"And you didn't bring it back?" she said. "What sort of man of science are you? *Sapere Aude!*"

"Whatever wisdom that's mine to seek lies in you."

"That's sweet. I love your poetic evasions but I don't believe them."

"Medicine is my excuse for using Latin phrases. What's yours?"

"Prep school."

"I see."

Sophia slipped through my arms, and with the water still running in the sink, left the kitchen with a glass of champagne in hand. I picked up the dishes where she had left off, allowing the repetitiveness of the chore to calm my mind. After restocking the cabinets and drawers with clean dishes I walked back into the living room to find Sophia sitting on the floor, her legs tucked to one side, leaning on one arm and turning the pages of our book with her free hand. Whenever she paused to sip from her champagne, the book, still quite stiff, closed shut and she would have to flip through to another place. I always liked this manner of sitting of hers, the way her supporting arm would eventually slide forward, widening the angle between her arm and body from acute to obtuse until she became a single, sinuous line. I found it both sensual and inviting, Sophia's elegant transition into recumbency. The late hour, the dim lighting, the unveiling of our book—these combined factors primed us for a rare occasion, a writhing, sprawling, and imaginative event, which took us to unexpected rooms, and finally, into a deep and dreamless sleep.

I awoke at exactly four a.m., completely lucid, and in a state of existential dread. This is something that happens to me from time to time. Occasionally at night, and more commonly after afternoon catnaps, I will jolt into consciousness from a complete void, and something, perhaps the abrupt transition between states, fills me with profound anxiety. My immediate reaction to this feeling is shallow but pragmatic: I read voraciously, work, or run. I do anything to convince myself that I am not living idly or in vain, even though, in my bones, there is an unspoken conviction that the papers and books around me are only trees, that the building I live in is only a rock, and that I am only some avid thing squirming in the cracks, destined like everything else to rot and vanish.

On this particular evening I didn't feel that running, reading, or working would do, so I took my wife's advice concerning my role in life as a scientist, and went back down to the dumpster.

I propped the lid, reached my arm in, and froze. I don't know why, but instinct prevented me from patting around or pushing trash aside in an attempt to search anything out. The same instinct had prevented me from bringing down a flashlight, or doing anything that would introduce intrusive or alien elements into this... home.

I kept my arm still and waited to see if the being would come to me. If it was as drawn to me as I was to it. After several minutes something warm and smooth nudged my fingertips. What began as a gradual, coiling ascent up my forearm changed into a sort of spreading (I don't know how else to describe it), onto my body. There were oddly spaced nubs and appendages, unmarked by claws or nails, which twitched and felt softly around my arm. Our eyes locked for a moment, and any of my residual fears were assuaged by the unmistakable intelligence and benignity of the beast. Once its body was completely out of the dumpster, it clung to me with all its weight and purred softly in my ear.

I returned to the apartment with my new discovery, cognizant of the fact that, to it, I was a new discovery. I entered the apartment quietly and, so as not to wake Sophia, avoided the bedroom and headed directly to a small sofa near the alcove facing the window. Sophia found us there in the morning, looking out at the city together, our twin skins reddened by the pigments of the sunrise. I looked up and saw amazement in my wife's face. Anyone else I knew, man or woman, would have screamed, but hers was the unwavering reaction of a true artist. She joined us on the sofa and we clasped hands together over this new thing between us.

"Female," I said. "That's about all I've determined at this point."

"Sapere Aude," Sophia said.

We called her 'Sapere' for short.

I went back to bed in order to catch up on missed sleep while Sophia stayed with Sapere in the alcove. When I woke up and emerged from our bedroom I found the two of them sprawling in a sizable square of sunlight quilted onto the hardwood floor. I made coffee and brought Sophia hers in her mug. She sat up to take it from me and I pulled up a stool alongside the two of them, and together Sophia and I sipped and talked in a manner typical of one of our lazy Sunday mornings, with the exception of the fact that, on this particular day, we both felt the excitement of being unexpectedly and abundantly blessed.

"I have a very distinct memory," I said, "of an afternoon in August, several days before I went into the first grade. Our dog, a mongrel, was lying in his favorite nook beneath the coffee table. I crawled up next to him and stared at his face for perhaps fifteen or twenty minutes. I had a rather strong attachment to this dog. I could feel his intelligence, and on several occasions I made painstaking efforts to teach him English so that he could tell me about his dreams. At any rate, what struck me that afternoon was the fact that there wasn't any great difference between his sensory organs and my own. I tried to imagine a creature of higher intelligence without a face, or without the features the dog and I shared, but I failed to come up with anything. It was like trying to invent a new color, or like trying to explain the beauty of music to someone born deaf. It's a feeling that has stayed with me and I think of it from time to time. But now, as I look at Sapere, I can't help but feel she is the very incarnation of that impossible being. The one I failed to imagine so many years ago."

"Mmm?" Sophia lay on the floor, her focus entirely on Sapere. "You were saying she has the most beautiful eyes?"

I didn't push the point. "Yes," I said. "They're beautiful. But beyond her eyes and skin, she is quite singular."

"Come closer," Sophia said. "I want to show you something."

I set my mug on the stool and knelt down beside the two of them. Sophia extended her index finger and made some rapid tracings on Sapere's skin. In flawless cursive that was purple edged in green, the sentence appeared, "Sophia loves Sapere." The words only lingered a few seconds before fading away. "Now," Sophia said, "you try." I held out my hand and spelled out in my ugly penmanship the first thing that came to mind: "What are you?" For some reason the color of my writing was different than Sophia's—orange rimmed in gray—but it faded just as quickly. Sapere purred with pleasure at experiencing human touch. It was clear that, whatever her experience had been prior to our spontaneous adoption, she craved and welcomed affection.

I was lost in these reflections when Sapere suddenly flinched violently, startling my wife and me, and moved in her cumbersome, idiosyncratic way to one side of the sofa, where we soon realized she was hiding from a large mirror propped against one of the pillars that supports the arch of the alcove. Neither Sophia nor I made any movement to comfort or retrieve Sapere, as we were curious to see how she might confront the dilemma on her own. Slowly she peered out around the corner of the sofa at her reflection, and, after several hesitations and a rather remarkable shift in her skin color from rosy to nearly violet, she summoned the courage to make her way toward the mirror. Once she was within about five inches, she stopped and studied her reflection. Her color returned to normal, and her respiration slowed notably. Before moving away from the mirror and coming back to us, she made several exertions which enabled her to wipe away a piece of rubbish clinging to her skin a few inches away from her eyes. This simple act immediately convinced us that she was sentient and self-aware to a very high degree, which was tremendous. It also alerted us to more obvious and practical considerations we had missed: after an untold amount of time living in the dumpster, Sapere, though mysteriously odorless, was in need of a good bath.

The month that followed was a honeymoon of sorts wherein I took a fairly unconventional leave from both my surgical practice and my position at the university. In the apartment, I pushed my carpentry skills to their fullest, constructing ramps and levers and a bizarre system of pulleys and wheels, compartments and drawers, steps and slides, something which resembled a dream-distorted miniaturization of some overly elaborate contraption which enabled Sapere to perform the basic functions of consumption, elimination, and recreation with relative ease. Sophia and I reveled in sharing those days together with Sapere, exposing her to our favorite cuisines and music and movies and wines and games; delighting in her awkward attempts to be like us and attending with prompt tenderness to the small lines of red paint and blood that bloomed from her skin whenever she attempted to wield our paintbrushes and scalpels. Never has there been a time in my life when I have felt freer or more fulfilled. And never has there been a time when I have been so blithe and courageous in pushing boundaries. As happened one night when all of us had perhaps one drink too many, my hand overlapped with Sophia's while caressing Sapere's skin. What can I say next except that what happened between us seemed so inevitable and also, so very natural.

I was on edge when I finally went back to work. All of the rituals and practices that had evolved among our trio had conditioned me to a different way of living, and I was not prepared for the shock of reentry into a work environment. I was distracted and irritable and had to summon all my concentration just to make it through a few minor surgeries without my mind wandering back to Sophia and Sapere. I felt that, trapped among people, I was missing out on a grander way of being; that I had ducked out of life for a quick nap and would awaken to find that I had missed out on the next tremendous step in evolution.

When I returned to the apartment I found the two of them just outside the alcove, Sapere positioned on a pedestal where the last rays of the day's light shone on her uncovered skin, and Sophia standing at her easel, painting her. It had been a day of frenzied artistic activity, as several completed oil canvases were already on display throughout the apartment. I felt betrayed that the two of them had instigated a new and intimate activity without my participation, and what's more, it was an activity which I could not participate in except as a passive observer. It seemed to me that Sophia had been waiting eagerly for an opportunity to do this, and that for quite some time she had been looking forward to my being away so that she could execute these paintings in my absence.

"Oil's a bit of a throwback for you, isn't it?" I said.

"Why's that?"

"Oh, I don't know. I seem to remember you saying it's passé as a medium, suited to the pretensions of a different era, or something to that effect."

"I don't remember that."

"Well, you said it."

"I don't deny that I did. I reserve the right to contradict myself."

"Of course. Forgive me. I suppose they're very good, for what they are."

For the first time since I had come home, Sophia stopped for a moment in her painting and looked up at me. "And what are they, Henry?" she said. "Since you're the art critic."

"Oh, come on now, Sophia. You know what I mean."

"Enlighten me."

"Please. Do I really need to say it?"

Her eyes widened and she shrugged, brush poised above the canvas, like a lever awaiting the switch of my speech.

"Fine," I said "They're pornography."

"Ha," she said, without laughing it.

"Listen, Sophia. This is exploitative, unimaginative trash, and we both know it."

She went promptly back to her painting with such concentration that it was as though she didn't even know I was there.

I left the room without a word and went to shower and change my clothes. When I came out again the sun had set and the canvas Sophia had been working on was propped against a wall. She had arranged Sapere in another pose and had illuminated her in the soft light of a small green lamp, and was fresh at work on yet another painting. I winced at the way Sapere looked upon the pedestal. She genuinely seemed to enjoy the adulation, but it cheapened her beauty, made her seem like something less than what she was. My heart ached.

The rift that opened between Sophia and me that night only widened. She couldn't resist showing the oils to her friends and they couldn't resist encouraging her. Soon the paintings were in galleries and the critics were abuzz. We hardly talked at home, but it was clear enough that she was enjoying the resurgence of her celebrity in the art world and that she wanted to believe that, unlike our book, the paintings of Sapere were a success that could not in any way be linked to me—this in spite of the fact that I was the one who'd plucked her muse from the garbage and brought her into the apartment. I was fond of cutting out sentences from certain reviews and posting them on the refrigerator along with little notes of my own. "Mann's hyper-realistic depiction of the decidedly unreal is truly original," wrote one critic. I added in the margin, "If only he knew that your true calling was that of a *portraitist*! How displeased you must be with this, as it slanders Sapere and makes a mockery of you."

This was typical of my vitriol, petty and cruel, and in retrospect, quite embarrassing. At one point I threatened to take Sapere from our home and offer her up to the medical community, which I argued we should have done in the first place, anyway. Sophia called my bluff and said that I would never want my diligent work as a surgeon to be overshadowed by a freak occurrence or chance finding. I denied the accusation that vanity was at the heart of my decision to keep Sapere a secret. I said we would only keep her for her own benefit, as the trauma of being taken from us and thrust into the public eye would no doubt be detrimental to her health and indeed might prove fatal.

———————

Things couldn't continue the way they were. We couldn't endure the arguments and sleepless nights and the poignant fearfulness and sadness of Sapere, her quiet gestures of affection and conciliatoriness which so devastated and humiliated us. I couldn't go on being so preoccupied with my home life that I put my patients in danger, nor was I willing to wager my career against consequences that could arise as a result. Things couldn't have been all that much better for Sophia. It is difficult to imagine that she would have been content to produce oil paintings of Sapere for the rest of her life. Sooner or later she would have gotten bored, and when Sophia becomes bored, it's only a moment more before she declares that she feels trapped. Then it's out with the old and on to another frivolous escapade. "Perpetual reinvention," she always called it. "Flight," I would say, or, if in the mood to exaggerate or (mis)diagnose, "dissociative fugue."

I won't pretend though, that the way in which I put an end to things was motivated in any way by a concern for Sophia's mental wellbeing. At the time I prodded myself on with the weak excuse that, as a man of science, it was my duty to do the thing I did for knowledge, for the good of mankind, for the perpetuation of the race. Of course, it wasn't any of that. It was a dark, nameless compulsion that I didn't understand then and am no closer to understanding now.

When I injected Sapere with the anesthetic, the matrix of her circulatory system flashed bright beneath her skin, the tangled net of her veins visible for a single second. She trembled but did not attempt to squirm away, her trust in me unshakable. I held my hand to her skin and waited for her golden eyes to close. When I knew she could not feel anything, I went to work.

Her muscles, sinew, cartilage, membranes, bones, veins, fluids, and viscera were unique but by no means revelatory. There was nothing there to merit the act I hadn't been able to restrain myself from performing. The prospect of carrying the bag down to the dumpster caused me profound anguish and guilt, so I found myself driving out to the countryside to a place where my father had taken me to fish in my youth. I knew of a special spot dense with clover and sweet grass, near a brook where it was easy to catch rainbow trout. Under the tangled weeds, a large stone still lay in the place where we buried my childhood dog.

By the look in Sophia's eyes I could tell she knew I was lying when I said that I had gone out to buy groceries and returned to find that Sapere had left without a trace. I could also tell that she was relieved.

We didn't speak for years after the divorce, until finally, after a phone call—I forget who called whom—we met in a cafe. Her hair was shorter and she had bangs. Living with her had accustomed me to her beauty and even enabled me to see some of the ugliness beneath it. The absence had freshened her, and I found myself envious of her new husband as we nibbled our scones and exchanged pleasantries. She had a wonderful, liquid laugh, and it made me feel charming to be able to incite it so easily once again. We found, but didn't say, that there were things we had loved about each other that we had forgotten but never stopped loving. Only fleetingly did we touch on one another's work. Neither of us mentioned Sapere. We hadn't worked out but we shared a special connection, like two people who awaken from fitful sleep and, after some discussion, realize they've shared the same dream.

Later that afternoon I disassembled the apparatus I had constructed for Sapere. I don't know why I kept it up for so long—nostalgia, penance, maybe just the simple inability to confront it. I felt an old pang in relegating the heap to the dumpster, then returned to my apartment to find that the floor was warped, unevenly sunned, and full of holes in the places where the apparatus had been bolted down. It left an imprint—a shadow, which to this day I find myself stepping around, unable to get accustomed to the space I have opened up for myself. I notice the same tendency near the alcove, where I duck to avoid the finest daylight, a habit I acquired in order to ensure that Sophia always had optimal conditions to practice her art. If I live here too much longer or allow too many others in, I will soon be crowded out entirely. The channels I move in are narrowing. At this rate the space will encroach inward until my home collapses completely, leaving behind only a rock and some trees. Then something else will take up residence, something other than the things that have come before it. It will stay and teem for a while and then it too will vanish. In a sense it already exists here, but I don't know what to call it.

The Sticking Place

Zana Previti

UC Irvine, MFA

When she found out that she was pregnant, my sister, Two, sent me a telegram: THE RABBIT DIED, it said, DUE CHRISTMASTIME. I hadn't been planning on returning to the United States for another three years. But then, a year or so later, a colleague of mine pulled out of his presentation at a Columbia conference, and the CDC decided to fly me back to fill in for him. I arranged to fly early into Dulles, and Two sent me a letter with lots of exclamation marks and photographs of their son: Henry Tan Pham. I was nervous, I remember, at the prospect of being so long in America. When I do return home, it's usually for a week of meetings, and then I'm back on a plane. I rarely have the opportunity to see my sister. I love her, but my life isn't over there any longer.

"Don't you ever think of getting married?" asked Two. We had packed Henry in what seemed like housing insulation, and he was stuffed immovably into his stroller. We were walking down Connecticut Avenue, to a bookstore near to their apartment.

"Of course," I said, "I *think* about it."

"Kids," she said.

"I don't really think I'd want kids," I said. "But this little man is very handsome."

"You *are* very handsome! Yes, my handsome man. It's so *cold*, but we'll be inside very soon. Do you really like it there?"

"In Tanzania?"

"In Tanzania."

"The sunsets are beautiful," I said.

"How often do you see a sunset?"

I held the door of the bookstore open, and Two wedged the stroller inside. She was younger than me by two years, and the second child. We never called her by her real name.

Two, her husband Vinh, and Henry lived high up on Connecticut Avenue, right on the D.C./Maryland border. I had a ten-day window before I needed to present at the conference, so I was staying with them in the apartment. Ostensibly I was there as a guest, but really, I wanted to help, so that Two could occasionally take a shower or read a book. Vinh worked very long hours downtown, and I was happy to clean and cook and do changings. I tried to do the shopping, but I was overwhelmed and upset in the grocery store. It was so big, and I was silly to try to be American again so quickly. But it was pleasant, actually, and refreshing to be around such a happy, healthy baby. Henry was fat and gorgeous. He tracked a finger beautifully. He didn't so much as sniffle.

I had work to do, of course, but there was a diner two blocks from the apartment building that was open twenty-four hours. I spent late nights there, working on my paper. Henry spent his night, from about 11pm–1am, participating in what Vinh called "ScreamFest" and so each night I did the dishes and cleaned the kitchen, and left the house by ten. I worked until 1 or 2am, and then returned to the apartment to sleep.

The diner was one of those fifties throwback places, with framed photographs of movie stars and cherry-red-chrome barstools. My waitress was a teenage girl named Katie. She had wispy blonde hair in a braid down her back and an overbite. Every night when I arrived I found her studying, hunched over a textbook with her elbows on the counter. She ran cross-country, she told me, and came to work at the diner right after practice. She had to hope for slow nights if she wanted to get her homework done.

"Dr. Porter," she said when I came in. She had seen my CDC nametag attached to my briefcase one night, and had since addressed me as Doctor. She sometimes sliced up a fresh strawberry for the top of my milkshake. Once or twice I was able to help her with her chemistry homework or a calculus problem. I was grateful, actually. It was rather fun doing molecular formulas again. And math! I loved math in high school.

"You have earned the right to call me Margaret," I told her, "Maggie, even."

"I like saying Doctor, Doctor," she said.

I worked at a corner booth underneath a gigantic framed poster of Marilyn Monroe executing a bench-press in a pair of jeans. Usually, I was alone in the diner; a few times, some rowdy folks would come in from the bar across the street, and Katie would seat them far away, so I could concentrate. It was a paper, I remember it very well, that I was presenting on mucocutaneous disorders in the children in Dar es Salaam. We had had some luck in using the dental lesions to help better understand what stage the disease had reached; often—usually—the children arrive with no explanation, and the most we can do is guess.

One night, Katie smiled an apology at me. A couple had come in just a few minutes before, she said, and they had asked specially for the booth I usually occupied.

The diner was quiet, though, and I waved it off and sat down with my work at the counter. I drank strawberry milkshakes as I worked, one or two a night. I love strawberry milkshakes, and since I was technically on vacation, I allowed myself the indulgence. One cannot get a strawberry milkshake in Tanzania. And somehow, when I am back in Atlanta, I don't really think of going out for milkshakes after a day of meetings. Perhaps I should.

That night, I worked for more than an hour until nature called me to the restroom. On my way back to my seat at the counter, I saw the couple still very comfortably occupying my booth in the corner. I saw, too, that the woman was uncommonly pretty, in just the way I appreciate most. She was wearing no makeup, and she had very dark, large eyes. It was cold outside, and she hadn't taken off her wool cap, which was thick and black and made her face look very pale. I am attracted to women, though most of my colleagues, I think, probably would be surprised to know it. Not, of course, that I've ever…done anything. I find it difficult to approach anyone with romantic intent. There was, once, in med school, a woman who worked in a lab down the hall from me, but we never actually spoke. To one another.

I suppose it was because I found the woman to be so attractive that I sat at the counter feigning work. From where I sat, I could see her face quite easily, but I could only see the back of the man's head. He had very red, curly hair, and when he shifted in his seat I could glimpse a thick red beard and mustache. The diner was so empty, and so quiet, that I could listen to their conversation without any effort. I had been wholly immersed in my work, to that point—I was writing, that night, an explanation of how the disorders would need to be described in the literature we planned to distribute for use in the clinical staging of the syndrome. Writing clearly is difficult for me. Complex thoughts seem to demand complex language, but I am drawn to simple sentences, simple vocabulary. Especially when the language is, as it was in this case, full of medical jargon. I can often rewrite a sentence ten times and be yet displeased. I was absorbed, as I said, or I should have heard them before.

"It's not as though you've decided on anything completely," the man was saying.

"I don't participate, Mike," the woman said.

"I don't know what that means."

"It means going out. Doing things. I don't even like it to go to the grocery store. Going for drinks. Going out to lunch. Being with people."

"I don't like those things, either."

"It's not that I don't *like* them, Mike. I do like them. I like this, coming out with you and eating food. But it's too hard…on the work. It takes me a long time to come back."

"I'm not asking you to go to a dinner party every night," said the man.

"Tonight I'll go back and stay up thinking of you, and for a long time a part of my mind will be preoccupied, turning *you* over and over, and I'll lose that part of my brain. If I keep my world very small, very contained, I can keep a tight hold on the character. But when I venture out I lose it a little, and it is always much harder to fight my way back in than it is to stay inside the whole time."

"I don't like many people, Blane. I don't like anyone. But you."

"You don't understand," she said. She picked up her hamburger and put it down again.

"Do you want the rest of my sandwich instead?" he said, "I do, actually. I do, because it's the same with writing. I hole myself up and ignore everything save bodily needs and I write. I get it. We're the same, and we've been the same our whole lives."

"Then you should understand that living with someone else would be fatal—to our work. No, I don't want it. You finish it."

"Not in the way we would handle it."

"To *my* work, then. You're established. You don't need as much. I'm still working."

"Did you know that I accidentally named three different characters in my new novel the same thing?"

The woman laughed. She had a throaty, deep laugh, as though she had been a smoker once.

"What name?" she asked.

"Guess."

The woman inclined her head to the side and reached her fingers underneath her wool cap to scratch behind her ear. She was very thin; the bones of her neck were very prominent.

"Man or woman name?" she asked.

"Woman."

"Elizabeth," she said.

"You will be successful, Blane. You will be. You're too good, and you work too hard. You're a beacon."

"I have a lot of doubt. I doubt a lot."

"Of course you do. But I've done it, Blane, and we're the same. We don't fail." She smiled at him.

"We fail?" she said. She said it as though she were making a joke. "But screw your courage to the sticking place, and we'll not fail."

"We can live someplace remote. In the wilderness. Build a house of sticks in the woods and ignore each other for weeks at a time, when we need to." He leaned over and started to eat the potato chips from her plate. She pushed it toward him.

"I like what we do now."

"What's that? See each other when our schedules accidentally intersect? Three times in two years? That's enough for you?"

"No, but it's appropriate. If we saw each other more, you'd come to agree, your writing would suffer. My acting would suffer."

"We're good at what we do."

"We are very good at what we do," she said. "Which is why we have to do it alone."

"I named them Liz, Bess, and Elizabeth."

"I think it's funny," she said. "You should keep it that way."

"Eat your burger," he said.

She frowned down at her food. "I can't," she said. "Too much."

"You're starving yourself now? You've lost weight since the last time I saw you. In London. And you were too skinny then."

"It's a cruel business," she said. "The stage lights are kinder to a thin face. I don't have cheekbones unless I'm at my birth weight."

He laughed.

At this point in their conversation Katie came over to me with a pained expression and a page of penciled calculus, and I spent a quarter hour with her. When we had sorted out that particular function of y, the couple had gone. I tried to write a bit more, but I found that my brain had reached its limit, at least as far as that was concerned.

A few days later, Vinh's parents took Henry for the weekend, to give the couple a little break. Two showered and changed her clothes and we went downtown, to the Folger, to see a matinee of *Macbeth*. We took the Metro, and when we stalled on the tracks Two groaned and stamped her feet like a child.

"I hate *delay*," she said. I didn't mind, though. It wasn't hot or uncomfortable in the subway car, or even crowded. We had seats next to one another. I am a patient traveler. Often, on planes, I'll be in my sweatpants, eating the little bag of pretzels, and I pretend that I am going some place nice. Paris, I sometimes imagine, with rain-wet streets and me, clean and dressed in black, hurrying to meet someone. Or a tropical island—*not* one devastated by a hurricane or tsunami—with a little breezy grass-thatched hut, with white gauzy curtains and a view of the sea. But not Africa. Not the pediatric centre in Dar es Salaam. I know many people don't like travelling, the grimy, stifling, getting-there part. They like to prepare, to pack, to buy and read colorful guidebooks and plan their days. And they like to arrive, to be swept away by the new smells and the strange food, to be greeted by people who love them and have been preparing for their arrival. But the process of *going* is an inconvenience. I have never felt that way. Sometimes the best parts of my journeys are the hours I spend in the air, getting there. I was going to say, the best parts of *my* life, but I shrink from something so…sad. And possibly untrue.

I didn't recognize her right away. She had been made up heavily, to look considerably older, and she wore an ash-blonde wig. When we look on a stage, we expect to see a stranger, a simulacrum of a person, and not a person. A fleshy body with wide eyes who sits in diners and wears woolen caps and won't eat her potato chips.

There were glimmers, I think, of recognition. When she first came on stage, she did a bit where she was reading a letter, and she was holding it up in front of her face. Then she sort of folded it up, like she was absent-mindedly making an origami bird, and she said, looking out at the audience, "*Thus* thou must do, if thou have it!" and I turned suddenly toward Two, as if something had happened, and I expected her to comment. But I did not know on what.

It was much later. Halfway through the play there was a scene in which a ghost came on stage—a man who Macbeth had killed. It was a dinner scene, with many characters, but Macbeth was the only one who could see this ghost. He was acting strangely, and no one could understand why, so Lady Macbeth was forced to make excuses for her husband. She had stood up, and she was standing so close to the ghost that they must have touched shoulders; the ghost had turned to look her in the face, but she did not turn to look back. The ghost's lips were so close to her lips; she would have been able to feel his breath on her skin, and yet she gave no sign. The lighting made her look very pale, and her eyes were very large, and I saw her, suddenly, that face I had seen in the diner. Not just the same woman, but more of her, if that makes sense—she was magnified, more alive and present than she had been in that small corner booth. I felt satisfied when I recognized her. And I was oddly happy to see her again.

At the end of the play, she came out on stage with the actor who had played Macbeth. They held hands and bowed together. She had kissed her fingertips and gestured to a place on the left side of theater. When I leaned to look where she was looking, I saw the redheaded man with the beard. He was standing, but not clapping like everyone else. He had crossed his arms on his chest and he was beaming at the woman on stage, smiling at her as though they were not far away from each other. As I watched, he held up one finger and he mouthed something—a word or a short phrase, and when I looked back at her, she had begun to cry. She put her hand over her mouth, waved once more at the audience, and the curtains closed. I had the sense that I had been a witness to something very private. It is, after all, sometimes possible to have deeply intimate moments even in the most public places.

I am so busy, every day, running from doctor to doctor, trying to make sense of test results and arguing with the government councils, spending hours trying to get someone from the CDC to approve a piece of equipment. We are concerned so much with saving the ones who can be saved that, too often, the sickest children get ignored. A Tanzanian doctor once told me that babies respond most to skin-on-skin contact, so if I can spare an hour I go to the nursery. We have dozens of newborns at any one time, most of whom die the week they arrive, and more arrive every day so the nursery is always noisy and bustling with volunteers and doctors and children. I keep a folding stool in the corner, and there I can sit and unbutton my shirt enough so that I can hold a little one against my chest. It is not my job. I direct the program, now. Sometimes I consult, but I have no real patients. They are such beautiful children, too, such beautiful babies. It is never enough. They live only a few days, and some never get held at all.

That night we sat out on Two and Vinh's little balcony, bundled up against the cold, because Vinh and I wanted to smoke cigars. We settled ourselves into plastic folding chairs, Vinh and I had our cigars and a couple fingers of whiskey, and Two had on a pair of fuzzy earmuffs. She was drinking cocoa, with two hands around the mug. Vinh laughed at her.

"You look about seven years old," he said.

"It's cold," she said to him. It was. I held my cigar with my right hand, and had to keep flexing the fingers to keep them from going numb.

We talked a bit about the play. Two hadn't liked the man who had played Macbeth. Vinh needed to be reminded of the plot.

"Oh, I remember," he said after I had tried to explain the plot and Two had succeeded, "The one with 'Out, damned spot!'"

"The woman," I said, "Lady Macbeth. I saw her, a few nights ago, at the diner. She was with a man and I thought she was very beautiful."

"You saw Blane Kronborg at the *diner*?" asked Two. "I don't believe it."

"Is it some big thing?" Vinh asked. The cigars were very good. I blew a smoke ring and Vinh nodded and blew one too.

"Blane Kronborg is famous," said Two. "I mean, not in the celebrity wedding-paparazzi way. But, really, she's very well known as a stage actress. Or, at least, she's getting very well known. Vinh, remember we saw her last year, when she was Pfeni Rosensweig?"

"No," said Vinh.

"Oh my word," said Two. "Yes, you do. When we were in Boston, and your mother's friend gave us tickets. Just after New Years? And you lost your car keys in the lobby."

Vinh groaned. "Oh my god," he said to me, "That was the worst night of my life. God. It was freezing. And we walked all the way back to the car before I realized they were missing. I almost punched the window of the car in. It was that cold."

"I've always wanted to try that," I said. "Wrap a t-shirt around my fist and break a car window."

"Right?" said Vinh.

"You are so gay," said Two.

I nodded. Vinh proffered his glass toward me, and I clinked it with mine.

"So who was she with?"

"Who?"

"Blane Kronborg," she said. "At the diner. Was she with anyone?"

"Yes," I said, "Some man. He was at the show, too. Very red hair, and beard."

"Oh my god," said Two. "She was with Michael Dunn. You saw Michael Dunn."

"Who is Michael Dunn?"

"I cannot believe you two," Two said. "Michael Dunn. He just won the Man Booker. For the novel about Mozambique. I gave it to you, Vinh, to read. Weeks ago."

"She gives me many things to read," said Vinh. He tapped the ash from his cigar into an ashtray and then handed it to me.

"It's very good," said Two. "I wish I was still at Tatnuck, so that I could teach it." Before they had decided to get pregnant, Two had taught English at a posh private high school in D.C. She'd hated it.

"No, you really don't," said Vinh.

"He's Canadian, I think. They were engaged," said Two. She had finished her cocoa and when she spoke, little tufts of her breath fogged before her face. "Two or three years ago. They met in Scotland, I think. Michael was writing his first novel there. It was about the Bruces. I didn't really like it much, but the Mozambique book is great. And Blane was there for some reason. I don't really know. Anyway they fell in love, and they were engaged, and he wrote this little play—and she was in it. I mean he wrote the play *for* her, a role special for her. It took off. Totally made a name for her. She was extraordinary, I take it. But he went back to writing novels, and he was researching his Mozambique book, and she was doing Cordelia in New York, and I guess it just…fizzled out. Long distance."

"How do you know all this?" asked Vinh. "Who are you?"

"That makes sense," I said.

"Why?" asked Two. "Jesus, it is freezing. Can you finish those things?"

"Just some things that they were saying," I said.

"Tell me immediately," said Two.

"You don't even know these people," said Vinh.

"Hey," said Two, "Be quiet."

Vinh brought his hand to his lips and appeared to lock them together with a small, invisible key.

"Give it to me," said Two.

He tossed it, and she caught it and put it into her pocket. It is a relief and a pleasure to see my sister happily married. I feel more comforted in the world. It can be, demonstrably, a nice place.

The next day was Sunday, and Vinh's parents returned Henry in the morning. I needed to leave in a few days, and the paper I was writing still needed quite a bit of work. I had been procrastinating certain sections. Really the dental symptoms were hugely overlooked, and still are. But my expertise is not in dental work, so explaining the signs and symptoms of lesions in the children's gums, and how to teach the local dental clinics to identify them, that was slow work. I had to get on the phone to a colleague in Atlanta more than a few times. The diner was loud and busy during the weekends, so I worked in the living room. I stretched out on the couch, typing with my computer in my lap.

Around noon, Two came in carrying a copy of Michael Dunn's book.

"Look what I found," she said, holding it out to me. "Vinh's not going to read it. Take it to New York. Read it on the train."

"Thank you," I said. It was a paperback. The cover was a close-up photograph of a goat's forelegs, in black and white. The knobby legs had been bound in a rope. I flipped the book open and read aloud, at random.

"But he did not. He was used to it. It had surrounded him since he had been a child. He found his way among his family, and the way was a way to indifference and, thus, to cruelty. Even when his inclinations pushed him in another direction—"

"It gets better," said Two.

"What do you know about him?" I asked. The cursor blinked on my screen. I closed it.

"Oh," said Two. "He's totally crazy. Totally. He used to teach. He was the one who resigned from Notre Dame—he was a professor there and resigned when they announced that Senator McCormick was going to give the commencement address. It was news. It was in the news. People know this stuff."

"I'd resign, too, if Senator McCormick was coming to my campus," called Vinh. He was in the kitchen, giving Henry a bath in the sink.

"You don't have a campus," laughed Two. "No eavesdropping."

"I'd resign from my job if we accidentally shared an elevator," said Vinh. "I'd get out of the elevator, go to my office, and type my resignation. The whole building'd be tainted."

"Anyway," said Two. "How's the paper?"

"Terrible," I said, and opened my laptop again. Two patted me on the shoulder, and for a moment, rested her chin on the top of my head. Then she left me alone to work. Henry was laughing, and I could hear his little legs splashing in the bath.

On my last night in D.C., I went to the diner. I wanted to drink a milkshake and to give Katie a big tip for all the nights she'd been so kind to me. I brought my work with me, but when I arrived I was in an odd mood. All I wanted to do was drink my milkshake, and do nothing: stare at the table, stare out of the window, watch the people walking by dressed to go out, the cars slowing down to get into the rotary. I took a seat at a table by the window, and left my computer and papers in my bag on the seat beside me.

Katie was carrying a plate of French fries to an elderly couple at the counter. She nodded at me, to show me that she had seen me and would bring my milkshake.

"I'm heading up to New York tomorrow morning," I said, when she came over. "Then straight back to Tanzania. So no more chemistry help, I'm afraid."

"Oh, Dr. Porter," she said. "I'll miss you! Who's going to keep me company?" She put the glass with the pink milkshake in front of me, and the cold tin cup with the extra bit in it. I do love milkshakes.

Katie watched me rip the straw from its little paper tube and put her hand out, to take it. "But I'm sure you're needed there," she said. "It must be very hard, seeing all those sick kids."

"Thank you," I said. She had sliced up a fresh strawberry and put two big pieces on the top of my milkshake.

"On the house," she said.

"Thank you," I said.

I sat there quite a long time, about as long as I would have if I had been working. It was a cold night, and everyone who walked by the window was bundled up in a puffy down coat and hat pulled very low. When Blane Kronborg appeared, like the ghost in the play, she stood and paused in front of the diner. I almost didn't recognize her, again. She was wearing one of those hats with the earflaps, and fur inside, and she had a black scarf wrapped about the lower part of her face. She stared, and those very large dark eyes looked, it seemed, right into mine. I admit I was thrilled, a moment, in spite of myself. She was, really, very beautiful. I know it's silly, but I had a sudden, wonderful vision, of she and I together. Somehow, I wouldn't go to Tanzania but instead buy a house, adopt a dog, lie in bed on Sunday morning with Blane Kronborg. I pictured her hand lying sleepily on my belly I pictured kissing her lips to say "Goodbye until later!" in the morning. I saw myself standing in the dark theater wings, watching her perform. There were no more dying children in my future, no more mosquito nets around tiny bodies that were too sick to cry, no more futility or helplessness or fatigue. I was with a beautiful woman. She was an actress, a serious actress; we went for milkshakes after her shows and then we went home. It was a little bit wonderful, really. I know how silly it is. But then, outside the diner, the figure in the hat and scarf put a finger up to her eyebrow, and I realized that Blane Kronborg had only been looking at herself, at her own reflection. She came in and seated herself, in the corner booth again, and I felt glad I had not taken it. She sat facing Marilyn, her back to the door.

He came about ten minutes later. He was wearing an overcoat, but no hat, and his hair looked wet and lay flat on his head. It made him look old. Old, but still attractive. They both had very good bones—faces that would age well and that betrayed their propensities to hard work and the pursuit of art. Like she had done, he paused in front of the diner and looked at himself in the window—steadily, again, so that it appeared as though he was looking at me. But unlike she had done, he did not rouse himself, did not put a hand to his face and come inside. He just stood there, with his hands in his pockets, staring at himself. I felt embarrassed for him, and yet I couldn't stop staring back. I was waiting, I guess, for Blane to turn around in the booth, to see him and wave him inside. But she didn't turn around. I think that's why she sat that way, so that she wouldn't see. I think she didn't want to be tempted. It must have been very cold outside. His eyes watered, and he wiped them with the end of his scarf; he must have been jarred from his contemplation that way, because when he looked back at the window he saw me. He smiled, rather boyishly I thought, and nodded. I nodded back, and then he turned around and walked off, south, down Connecticut Avenue. And just then I felt very sad and very happy at the same time. I felt very close to them, though that may seem strange. But I did. I felt very close to the both of them.

Henry is almost six now and starting kindergarten. I haven't been back to the States and I won't be back again, I don't think, for years at least. The Centre has received some generous funding and we're expanding. I really can't spare the time to go back. Two writes me letters that end with the phrase, "We miss you!" but I am unable to write this in my own letters to her. I don't miss America, or the people there. I don't mean I don't love them. I do. But to miss something must mean that you feel it, consistently, an ache or throb where something vital has been wrenched away. I have no such ache. I work, all the time. It is the strange contradiction of my life, that I despair at my work but love deeply the work itself. If something is missing, if something has been taken that I need, I can't feel it.

I still think of them, and wonder about them. I hope they are both well, and happy. That they have healthy children together, if they wish for children. Or that they are able to see each other, at least, once every few years, and able to take some joy in those meetings. It's a nice thing for me to think about, something very soothing for me. I know that, because they are both well-known people, I could easily look them up the next time I get to the internet cafe in town. I won't, though. I'd rather spend some time, every day, thinking about them, and imagining their happiness.

Wellspring

K.M. Ferebee

The Ohio State University, MFA

They had been three weeks upon the expedition. Gris woke now in the night, just before dawn, some days, and watched the red line of the sun on the horizon, and could not remember rain upon his face, nor the faience blue of the sea where it touched the raw coast of his green-drenched home in the Indies.

It had rained on the day that they left Laada: a fey, light, and glittering rain that glazed the rooftops and stood out like sweat on their bodies. Meo had turned the cuff back from his wrist and held his arm out, then put his mouth to his skin, tasting the water. Gris had watched him. Meo had said, "I can taste the desert in this." He'd licked his lips, a quick animal flicker of tongue. Since then, rain had ceased to exist. There was only the eggshell dome of the sky, bleached like a bone that sun has scavenged.

There were four of them: Gris and Meo, and the two native men whose language Gris did not speak and Meo spoke a little. The men wore white cloth and carried rifles. They eyed Gris and Meo contemptuously. In the evenings they prayed, bent close to the sand, their bodies nearly prostrate. Their form of prayer had a particular cadence, rising and falling, which Meo would sometimes imitate when he and Gris were lagging behind. He fitted his own syllables to the recitation, and Gris could not tell if they had meaning. He understood that what Meo did was not mocking, but he was troubled by the mimicry. He said, "Don't. I don't like it. You don't know what you're summoning." Meo glanced at him from under solemn dark lashes; lowered his gaze. He whistled a cryptic phrase of music. The air of the desert muted it fast. After a moment he whistled it again.

Meo had the olive skin and the high, dark features of someone born to hot climates. The sun did not burn him, or rarely. He wore his white shemagh like a native. In Laada, he had sometimes been mistaken for a native. Men and women would stop him on the street and speak to him in their liquid, circling language. He would spread his hands and say a phrase that meant (he told Gris), "Go more slowly, please" or "I am a stranger." These men and women would not talk to Gris, who was pale and had hair the color of fox fur. If pressed to pay him some attention, they would preface their remarks to him with a covering of the eyes: a gesture, Meo told him, that protected against *mal de ojo*. Gris said, "I don't know what that means." Meo laughed, and muttered something in Spanish. Later he showed Meo, in the deserted courtyard of a restaurant, a dead white tree into which some unknown hand had carved the shape of an eye. Pieces of Laadi money were tied to the branches of the tree with ribbons, and blue glass amulets hung, pendulous, in the breeze. "*Mal de ojo*," Meo said. "Evil eye." Gris examined the carving, touched the tree. The trunk was smooth and hollow, withered. The cuts were deep.

The fever revisited Gris on the twenty-fourth night of their journey. At first he thought that it was only sunstroke, which he had very often suffered in the early part of the expedition, but as the night progressed he began to sweat. Perspiration dampened the skin of his hands so that his palms left black prints on the blanket. He turned from one side to the other, paralyzed by fear, afraid to sleep. The episodes of fever often presented with dreams of disorientating clarity. Colors in these dreams were oddly heightened. Smells haunted him for days after waking. At home in the Indies, in the first fits of sickness, he had once dreamed that he was standing in a garden, beside a single fountain that had ceased to flow. Lichen made the surface into an island, matted and startlingly green. To his left was a lemon tree. Its branches were drooping. He could smell the leaves, bruised and sweet, as though after a thunderstorm. Thirsty, he dipped his hand into the fountain, hoping to find clean water to drink. Instead he felt something move against his fingertips, down under the green lichen, where he could not see. The horror of this dream stayed with him. For a long time, he felt physically sick each time he smelled or tasted lemons. He had overcome the reflex by the time he came to Laada, with its superfluence of citrus trees. But the scent of them that hung in the city gave him headaches.

Now his shuddering woke Meo, sleeping some feet from him. Meo sat up. In the firelight, his eyes gleamed. "*¿Enfermo?*" he asked, before he had quite adjusted. English was not the language in which Meo dreamed. Then: "Are you ill?" He shifted his blankets, and crept along the sand till he could cup Gris' face. The sweat ran at Gris' forehead like water. His hair was soaked with it. A heat rose off him that seemed inhuman. He wondered how Meo did not flinch. But Meo merely sat in the sand cross-legged and stripped off his shirt, applying it as a compress. It felt mercifully cold. The cloth smelled of Meo, clean and faintly musky. Gris closed his eyes. He heard Meo sigh. "The sweating will be gone soon. It will be morning. The stars are moving. In the desert you can see them all. I will tell you their names," Meo said. He began to outline the constellations, not ones with which Gris was familiar. There were the Dhow and the Dromon, low ships that sailed toward the horizon. There were the Dark-Eyed Girl and the Singing Imam, names that Meo would not further explain. The sound of Meo speaking was a current that Gris let carry him to the frontier of sleep but no further, so that when dawn came, he was still listening.

Meo had sat with him many times before, through such fevers. "Fevers," though they were all children of the same fever: a sickness that he carried in the blood, in his body, from place to place. He had got it in the Indies—a surfeit of damp air in childhood, claimed one doctor. Another blamed the quantity and nature of his dreams. A third doctor spoke of insects that thronged against the windows of Indian houses nightly: lustrous and winged, darkly writhing, the bearers of disease. Gris had been bled by all of these doctors, dosed with mercury and quinine. He had visited shamans in villages on his native island who had led him into the jungle and bade him to drink strongly spiced, vegetal-smelling decoctions while they danced around him in a cacophony of bells and hollow wooden clappers. They mimed pulling a demon out of him: hand over hand, as you would reel a fish from the sea. Lastly they coaxed a bird down from the forest, out of the tar-black canopy: a fist-sized bird with blind white eyes that blinked rapidly. Gris lay perfectly still. The bird alighted on his chest. He felt its small feet like the scratch of writing, like a sharp nib against a sheet. The bird wandered to the left part of his ribcage. It stopped above his heart, and began to drive its beak into the skin. Blood welled up, or perhaps Gris had dreamt this. Later his chest was unmarked, but he did not quite believe it. He remembered the bird's eyes, smooth and blind, twitching back and forth as though searching.

It had been Meo who suggested travelling to the spring. He had come across a reference to it in some antique book. Or had he encountered its mythology on some previous visit to Laada? It was difficult to recall. They had been living in Ludminster at the time, Meo working as a translator, Gris a recent migrant from the Indies. Gris remembered the day: a cool and rainy morning, maps spread out across the breakfast table, pictures of minarets and the moon above sand-dune mountains. Meo spoke about the desert reverently: "A strong wind will erase your footsteps as though they had never been, so that those who live there believe you must have a guiding spirit, a private jinn, the purpose of which is just to take you where you are going. Every person, they think, possesses this. It is the only way to resist losing one's way in the desert." Meo purported to know a great deal about these things, but he did not let on if he believed them. He pointed out names on the map and translated their meaning: the Plain of a Thousand Ghosts, the Grave of the Almond Khalif, the Red Gate of Ravenous Men. There were stories behind each that Meo did not tell him. Laada, Meo said, meant "the shell-like city." When he said it, Gris did not think of damp seashells, but of paper locust skins.

On the twenty-fifth day, they resumed the expedition. Gris' fever had gone from him. This was in the nature of the sickness: it came at night and then went in the day, repeating the cycle, sometimes for weeks. Gris would awaken exhausted, wrung-out and sore, and want to sleep till sundown, when the shivering began. Now he did not yet feel it much. He was able to keep pace with Meo, if not with the native men. He etched his spindly stride across the high dunes. He did not turn to see the wind efface it. He continued walking till sometime after noon, when one of the native men called out: a curt word to one of his fellows. "What is it?" Gris asked. Meo, looking ahead, said, "It is nothing. They are seeing mirages." Gris crested the dune and cupped his hands above his eyes, his feet sinking in the sand as he did so. The light was like a cloud that hung over the desert. The line of the horizon moved. It crawled, a slow serpent, a long, sinister, living thing. One of the Laadi men gestured to Gris; he pointed and said a word, trying to make Gris understand. Gris looked back again and saw an almond tree growing in the infertile sand. The tree was in blossom, green fruit just beginning to bear down each black-barked, whippy branch. White-pink flowers, pale and skin-colored, persisted. As he watched, a slow wind stirred through it. Cool shadows patterned the ground, inviting him. Without thinking, he stepped toward it. Meo stopped him. "It is a mirage," he said. "The desert makes them." Gris glanced back. Meo asked, "What do you see?" Gris described the tree, its dark branches. Meo said, "Some men see the minarets of cities, some see oases guarded by angels; still others think that they see the sea." His eyes were fixed on the space where Gris had been looking. He shifted the weight of his pack and said, "One can distinguish a fantasy. For instance, it is not the right season for almonds." As he moved on, the sun stretched his shadow till it was a narrow path of darkness on the desert's surface, unfolding like a wing.

On the twenty-sixth day, they reached the area where Gris had seen the almond tree, or such was his estimate. It was evening, the black edge of the earth bisecting the sun. In the place where the tree would have been was a pile of rocks, weathered clean, each about the size of a grown man's skull. There were in total perhaps twelve or thirteen. Gris hefted one. It was hot to the touch, which surprised him. A whisper went up between the two Laadi natives. Meo said, "They say this is a grave, the place where a dead man is sleeping." Gris placed the stone back hastily. "Don't worry. You can't give offence," Meo told him. "They think you are like a dead man already. You are unclean." "Can't you explain to them?" Gris asked, his voice rising a little. He was disturbed. He felt that the superstition in some way changed, affected him. He was marooned by his own lack of understanding. The men looked at him constantly from the corners of their eyes, as though he were someone they pitied. They would not eat with him, nor share his water. They would not even tell him their names. *Mal de ojo*, he thought. Meo said, "It is beyond my fluency."

They camped that night beside the grave. The Laadi men would sleep no nearer than several meters. Their separate fire made Gris uneasy. He would see it stir at the periphery of his vision and mistake it for a ghost, a jackal, a jinn, and his heart would jump even as he was comprehending that it was only the wind. Meo said, "You are getting superstitious. Perhaps you would rather sleep like them, out in the desert." In fact, Gris had thought to suggest it, but he did not now want to give credence to this teasing. Instead he set his bedroll down beside Meo's and lay in it. The long light of the fire reddened his eyelids. He felt Meo lie down beside him. Meo said, "When you're with me, there is nothing for you to be afraid of." He curled his arm over Gris' shoulder possessively.

Gris slept, and in a fever dream, saw one of the many bathhouses of Laada where men in wooden shoes slipped in and out of hallways through clouds of fragrant steam. For a price, a bathhouse attendant would take a cedar switch and beat you clean, the cut fronds streaming lukewarm water. In the languid heat, Gris could doze and imagine the liquid noises he heard were those of his home in the Indies. Yet here was Meo, coming to shake him awake and lead him through the tiled corridors to a room he had not seen. Meo was barefoot, leaving faint, high-arched prints against the stone flooring. He wore a towel wrapped twice around his waist. His upper body was bare, and Gris noticed for the first time a forest of white scars covering his skin. They were fine as filaments, visible on both the chest and back—sometimes straight as though from a whip-stroke, sometimes coiled like a dense cursive script. Gris stopped. He gently touched Meo's shoulder, tracing one knotted cicatrice. He felt nauseous, uncomfortable. He wasn't sure what to do. The blind, white scar tissue sickened him. The wounds spoke of some stained past, painful and violent; the sort of past that sears and deforms, the sort that bleeds. Abruptly, the wet air of the bathhouse was oppressive. He wanted very much to leave. But Meo said, "No, we are not there yet." He seemed oblivious to Gris' horror. He turned and smiled, lowering his long dark lashes. For a second he was so desirable that Gris could scarcely breathe. "You'll like where we're going," he said. "I promise. You'll see."

Gris woke chased by an echo of nausea from the dream. He leaned over and retched emptily. His blankets were soaked with sweat. Beside him, Meo was still sleeping. Dawn prowled the outskirts of the dark air; from the far camp he heard one of the men speaking. His hushed voice shivered in the silence. Gris strained to hear, but stayed uncomprehending. Meo moved, pressing his face into the bedroll, drowsily protesting. For a moment Gris watched him. Without letting himself think, he reached out and drew back Meo's shirttail. He trailed his fingers down the smooth whole skin beneath it. He closed his eyes; saw phantom scars. He let his hand rest on Meo's ribcage.

The spring was now three days distant, if their maps were to be believed. Neither the native men nor Meo would commit to this figure. The spring was not a city, it was not a caravanserai; both of these were locations more or less fixed. The spring, on the other hand, was supernatural in nature. It might go where it pleased. Gris was troubled by this response. Meo shrugged and said equanimously, "It isn't as

though we are in a hurry. We have supplies, and no particular need to return."
"Yes, but…" Gris found it difficult to pinpoint his distress, the sense that this idea seemed unreasonable. He felt groggy and sun-sick. He said, "I will be glad when we leave the desert." Leaving was a thing he could not imagine. He associated it with the touch of rain, the feathery sound of the sea.

In Ludminster, Meo had located the spring on a sequence of maps: some showing topographic features, others political boundaries. "So far is it within the desert, they say, that a man may die without reaching it. But he who drinks from it will forever after be free of all disease." Gris was dubious. Despite his upbringing in the myth-thick Indies, he had an erratic sort of faith, indifferent on the topic of miracles. He believed in luck and superstition, but miracles he found difficult to believe. "Where I come from," Meo said, "we have such places. We do not speak about them. Shrines where saints have died, where bones of saints are buried. I have personally seen a bird descended from that flock of San Cuervo. Do you know the story? It is a *misteria*, the story of a martyr. The man was murdered in Beget at the behest of a kalif. The kalif wished San Cuervo's heart to be cut from his body and pierced by a staff, a warning to Christians. His soldiers split the ribs, searched in the bloody part of the chest, down in the chest cavity, but when they pulled out what they thought was the heart, it spread little wings. It was a bird that slipped their bloody hands. Again they searched—gore up to their elbows—and produced a second heart, red, warm, and wet, and again it sprouted wings. You can imagine how this continued: till there was a flock of birds, all smelling of flesh, filling the rafters." Meo's fingers fluttered briefly outwards. He had exceedingly beautiful hands, Gris had often thought, long and expressive. It was distressing to think of them wet and blood-covered, like the birds' wings. "These birds," Meo said, "are reputed to have power. They live forever, and have great force of healing." Gris asked, skeptical, "Are you supposed to ask the bird to heal you?" Meo looked as them as though he were stupid. He said, "You kill the bird and clean its bones. Keep them in a little box. A…how do you call it? A reliquary." Gris felt slightly sickened. He looked at Meo's hands, closed now in fists. He thought of how easy it must be to kill a bird, barehanded. Imagined the beating of its heart against his fingers, the frantic scratching of its little feet.

It had seemed then that Meo had some secret knowledge, some source of power—savage and innate—that Gris was required to trust without real apprehension. Meo had been insistent: "We must go to the spring. You will not ever be well without it. You've seen the doctors; they have nothing to tell you. The fevers will not cease." And Meo had plotted their course—from Ludminster to Le Havre, and thence overland, through the Levant, passing Cappadocia and Greece. Meo had previously visited all of these places. He possessed a store of knowledge about each. The correct sites to cash checks or change money, the quiet cafes, the stylish hotels, the chapels where you could see Old Masters if you asked the priest. In Venice they had rented a boat, and Meo poled between the buildings, down silent alleys of water where the city seemed asleep. Then, abruptly, he would tie the boat to a stop, and lead Gris up stairways half-sunk in grimy water into arcane palazzos forgotten, apparently, by all other explorers. There was a strong drowned smell in each of these places, and in one palazzo, Gris had found watermarks on the wallpaper as high as his head. "Marvelous, isn't it?" Meo had asked, as they stood in a courtyard of an eighteenth century mansion. Gris had trailed his fingers along the rim of a fountain. Some five or seven carp troubled the water within. The water was brackish. The fish blindly sought the surface with eyes the same white-gold color as their skin.

In Laada, it was traditionally believed—or so Meo said, without attributing a source for this assurance—that water was the province of ghosts and jinn. Superstition attached itself to rare summer rainstorms, even to the dripping of a sink. The latter was a sign that ghosts were entering your house. It indicated flaws in your spiritual fortifications. There was an ancient belief that angels were attracted to wells and would wait beside them, disguised as travelers, until offered a sip of water. At this point they revealed their splendor and vanished. Their purpose was the will of God, and therefore cryptic. Perhaps, Gris said, they just wanted a drink.

It was true, he would admit, that the Laadis fought wars over wells, and believed in blessing oneself before touching water. Their bathhouses hummed with incantation. These were the preoccupations of a drought-bred people. He didn't accept there was any great secret to the thing. "Think of all the water, even in the desert," he'd said to Meo. "It can't all be haunted, or even cursed. You'd be overrun by ghosts, every day." Meo had looked at him with suppressed amusement. "Spoken like a person who comes from the sea." Gris had wished to point out that he'd not lived in the midst of the ocean, on an atoll or a reef. A sudden image had come to him of the Indian coast: the blue waves clawing landwards, the tangle of rot and green where mold coalesced on every surface. When the fever took him in the desert, the salt taste of sweat made him think of the sea. He said to Meo upon waking, "I miss the ocean." Meo stared into the flat horizon, unblinking. He said, "They say that in the heart of every desert is a well that goes to heaven. The water drawn from it is pure; its source cannot be seen. Superstitious men, or those damned by sin, used to dive into it, hoping to reach paradise." "And what happened?" Gris asked. "They drowned and the well was poisoned by their bodies. Imagine, the stench." Meo stood. He said, "That is one way ghosts get in the water." He did not enumerate the other ways.

On the twenty-eighth day, they reached the last well on their maps. The terrain from here out was a mystery. This well, it was communicated to Gris by Meo, belonged to no clan or tribe. No one would claim it. Clay bricks, mud-baked, denoted its border. The outline of an eye was etched roughly into each. Meo pried loose one of the bricks from its mortar. He held it in two hands, thoughtfully. One of the native guides spoke to him with force. Gris watched, not comprehending. Meo replied in the same language. Gris asked, "What did he say?" Meo said, "He recommends that we not drink the water." The man spoke again, gesturing to Gris. "You may drink the water," Meo corrected. "You are already unclean." Gris said, "I wish you would not say that." He walked to the edge of the well and peered in. The well was narrow and dark. He could not see its terminus. He said, "Hand me a water skin. I'll lower it." Meo uncapped a water skin and gave it over to Gris' outstretched hand. Gris inched it downwards on the well's long rope. He felt rather than heard when touched the rim of the water: the sudden weight, the skin's expansion. He waited, letting the water fully fill it. The sun beat down upon him. The native men backed off from the well. They were talking to each other, their tone uneasy. Gris did not like the way they looked at him, as though he were bleeding from the nose and mouth, or suffering from snakebite. As though he were already dead. He lifted the water skin up from the well. It was heavy. He took the skin in his hands and drank straight from it. The water was cold and tasted ancient. He tried not to think how deep the well must be. He swallowed. Then again, wiping his mouth. When he offered the skin to Meo, Meo backed away. He still held the clay brick, its black eye staring upwards. Meo said, "You drink. I'm not thirsty."

That night, the sky was clotted with stars. Gris said, "Tell me a story. To stop me feeling cold. To stop me getting ill." Meo thought and said, "Have I told you the story of the homa bird and the king who caught it?" "No," Gris said. Meo said, "There was a king. He went out hunting, and he struck a homa bird. This is a holy bird, which has no feet, which from its inception is air-bound, never touching the earth. The king caught the bird as it fell, and saw that it was dying. The arrow had pierced its heart, just—" he gestured to his own heart, "here. The wound would not be undone. The king saw that it was holy. He fell to his knees, crying, *O God, if it be written, let me take the place of the bird.* Upon which the breath of God moved him, and he took up his sword, and severed his own feet. Then he was like the bird." Meo stared at the ground. His expression was shadowed. "He became a holy man. Peace be upon him." Gris asked, "And the bird?" "It died," Meo said. "What do you think happened?" The thought seemed to distress him. His ember eyes burned.

They slept some distance from the fire, after Gris complained of its heat. It was incalescent, its force increasing in waves that beat against his sanded skin. Yet later, he begged to be thrown in the fire. His teeth chattered. He shuddered. Meo, with all the strength in his slight body, held him back. It seemed to Gris that Meo spoke to him for a long time in Spanish, and then in another language that Gris did not speak, and told him a wandering, incoherent story about a dying bird and a white birch tree. Still, later: "Do you remember?" Meo asked him, "when we met? What you said to me?" Gris thought. They had met some years back, by Gris' large and ramshackle house in the Indies. It had been summer, and so hot that flowers wilted on their branches, birds had fled to the jungle, and the air was seeping. By the water pump in the garden—a bulky, antiquated object—Gris had seen Meo squinting at the sun, carrying a canvas rucksack. He had run short of water out in the forest; he'd been sightseeing. "Could I use your well?" he'd asked. He had smiled, disarming. His dark hair had been flat with sweat; he was filthy, and a faint accent had colored his speech. "It's only an old water pump," Gris had said. "Let me get you something to drink." He said it now, repeating it, though he had forgotten Meo's question. Toward morning he slept a little, fitfully, and woke to find Meo tracing his face with one finger. Gris flinched. For a second, he thought he was dreaming. Meo said, "*Tranquilo. Cálmate.*" Tired, Gris let his head drop back. He said, drowsily, "You've been crying." He could see salt tracks on Meo's face.

When dawn came, he woke alone to find Meo waiting. Their bags were already packed. Their guides were not to be seen. "They've gone in the night," Meo said. "They were superstitious." Troubled, Gris looked for the men's footprints, as though it were not too late to trace them. He said, "But how will we make our way back? With just the maps—" Meo cut him short. He said, "Don't worry about these things." Then, as Gris tried to stand and faltered: "Let me help you. We're not far from the spring." Gris let Meo help him up. Then, while Meo folded and stowed the blankets, he forced down a mouthful of water from the skin. The water tasted different now, as though mixed with ashes. He saw mineral flakes in it when he poured some in his hand. Meo said, "We must leave, to make it by sundown." He eyed the water skin, but did not drink.

They walked without speaking. The sun wore on. Narrow hills rose here and there like pillars. Their rock was dark and red, and offered little shade. Nevertheless, Gris and Meo stopped just below one in the later part of the day. Gris sat in the cool, small spot of darkness. Meo seemed impatient. He shielded his eyes, looked toward the horizon. Gris swallowed water and felt weak, chilly. He asked, "Can you see the spring from here?" "Yes," Meo said. But Gris saw nothing when he stood to look. He shouldered his pack and started walking. Meo followed, a pace delayed. "Tell me the story of the spring," Gris said. "It will pass the time till we reach it." "There is no story to the spring," Meo said. He was looking straight ahead. "No saints?" Gris asked. "No birds? No kalifs?" "No," Meo said.

Just before dusk, Gris heard a high fluting: a note of music in the air. He touched Meo's arm. He said, "Listen." "Yes, I know," Meo said. They rounded one of the red rock hills. There, in the desert, was a stooped white tree. Its trunk was dry and smooth and knotted. Gris could not identify the species. It bore no leaves, but onto its branches someone had tied small objects: bronze coins, some centuries old by their look, and patterned cloth, and clay beads. The fluting Gris had heard came from bones, whittled down so the wind whistled emptily in them. He touched one of the bones. It might have come from a jackal, or a bird; he could not tell if it was human. He said on impulse, "We ought to leave something." Meo considered. "Yes," he agreed. "Give me your pocket knife." Gris did so. Meo reached out and touched his hair lightly. He brought the knife to the side of Gris' head and severed a lock of red hair. He took a string from his pocket and tied Gris' hair to the tree. He was still holding the knife in one hand, careless, and after a moment Gris said, "You're bleeding." "Am I?" Meo checked his hand. A long cut ran down the length of his palm. The cut was not deep. Meo pressed his hand against his mouth, just for a moment. When he moved it there was blood on his lip, on his teeth. "A slip of the knife," he said. Gris did not like the sight of blood, and suddenly he did not like the tree, with its bowed and twisted trunk, its bone ornaments, his own fox-colored hair bright red against the branch. "Please," he said, "let's leave." Meo looked at him in surprise. "But we're here," he said. "We're here. This is the spring."

Gris looked. He saw a large red rock about three meters from the tree. It was sickle-shaped and cleft in two by the water that ran from it in a dark stream. The water appeared to well directly from the rock. It was this water that fed the tree. There was no sign of a shrine. The sand was not disturbed. He and Meo might have been the first to set foot there, were it not for the offerings left on the tree. He said, uncertainly, "Are you sure?" But, compelled by the ceaseless line of water, he was stepping forward already. He had not been cognizant of his thirst. Now it opened like a wound within him, and all at once he longed to drink. Behind him Meo stirred, and reached out to touch him. Gris brushed him off. He could think only of thirst. He knelt down by the spring, extending his hand to catch the water as it snaked across the rock. The water was cold against him. He bent his head to drink. Behind him, Meo said, "I'm so sorry." His voice was pitched low with nervous despair, a kind of suffering. Gris turned to look at him. Sun rent the thin white curtains of sky. Meo stood amid it. The sunlight silhouetted him with luciferous splendor; a kind of glory so searing that Gris could barely locate him. He saw the bright ambit of Meo's body, bordering darkness. His thirst displaced all other thoughts. Once again, he turned toward the spring. Its winding dark line cut a word in the sand, a word he wished he could read. The smell of water rose up and overwhelmed him. Desire rose up inside him, spread its wings.

Acknowledgements

The Masters Review would like to thank the ten published authors in this collection. Thank you for your wonderful stories and for allowing us to showcase your talent. We're extremely proud of your work and honored to include it. Many individuals were responsible for the making of this review and an even greater number of people provided unwavering support. The Masters Review would like to formally thank the following individuals: Lauren Groff, Justin Curzi, Joy Uyeno, Nikki Volpicelli, Kelly Garrett, and Mackenzie Griffith.

CPSIA information can be obtained at www.ICGtesting.com
Printed in the USA
BVOW021721040612

291745BV00005B/1/P